THE DOMINATRIX

Also by Emma Allan published by X Libris:

The Disciplinarian

THE DOMINATRIX

Emma Allan

LIBRIS

X LIBRIS

First published in Great Britain in 2000 by X Libris
This paperback edition published in 2010 by X Libris

A CIP catalogue record for this book
is available from the British Library.

ISBN 978-0-7499-5471-0

Printed and bound in Great Britain by
Clays Ltd, St Ives plc

Papers used by X Libris are natural, renewable and
recyclable products sourced from well-managed forests and certified
in accordance with the rules of the Forest Stewardship Council.

Mixed Sources
Product group from well-managed
forests and other controlled sources
www.fsc.org Cert no. SGS-COC-004081
© 1996 Forest Stewardship Council

X Libris
An imprint of
Little, Brown Book Group
100 Victoria Embankment
London EC4Y 0DY

An Hachette UK Company
www.hachette.co.uk

www.littlebrown.co.uk

The Dominatrix

Chapter One

KAREN MASTERS SLOTTED the video into the machine, picked up the remote control and made herself comfortable on the Miltons' big, cream-coloured sofa. For the first time since she had come to stay with them a month ago they had left her alone in the house, and she was looking forward to a night on her own.

Karen had arrived in London from Devon to take up a new job and had needed somewhere to stay while she looked for a place of her own. The Miltons had offered to rent her a room at a very reasonable price. They used to have a country cottage near her mother's house in Christchurch, and her mother had always kept an eye on it for them. Though they had sold the cottage a year ago they were glad to be able to do something positive in return, they said.

The Miltons would not be back till late, she knew. They were going to a charity ball at the Grosvenor House Hotel. Karen had selected *Love Story* from their large collection of pre-recorded videos because she felt like something mushy and sentimental. She pressed the play button and reached for her glass of red wine. The bottle Barbara Milton had opened for her before they went out stood on the coffee table beside the glass.

1

Karen watched as the television set flicked into life. For a moment she was puzzled. Instead of the expected opening credits and haunting music, the screen was showing a small, square room. The walls were grey as was the carpet but there was no furniture. Instead, in the middle of the room was a vertical metal frame, painted black, from which hung a number of chains and leather straps.

This was clearly not the opening sequence to the Hollywood classic. Karen got to her feet and began to walk towards the video recorder. But as she reached for the eject button a tall, slender woman appeared on the screen, walking towards the metal frame with her back to the camera. She had sleek long black hair, pinned into a chignon on her head. She was wearing a red satin basque with long red suspenders clipped into sheer and shiny black stockings and red satin thong-style panties, no more than a thin strip of material that cut deeply into the cleft of her bottom. Her red patent leather stilettos had a spiky four-inch heel, which firmed the muscles of her legs and tightened the curves of her pert buttocks. Her arms were sheathed in a pair of skin-tight red satin gloves that reached all the way up to her armpits. The woman stood by the frame and began unbuckling the leather cuffs that were attached to short chains at each corner.

Karen found herself staring at the screen with fascination. But as the woman turned to face the camera, her fascination turned to astonishment and embarrassment. She felt herself flush a deep red. The woman was Barbara Milton.

The bra of the basque was no more than two crescent-shaped cups of material which lifted but did not hide Barbara's breasts, which were large and round with wide, dark bands of aureole and big cherry-sized nipples. The nipples stood out prominently, puckered and erect.

Squatting down, Barbara unbuckled the two cuffs at the foot of the frame. Then she straightened up slowly and raised her right hand, crooking her index finger to beckon someone in.

Immediately Dan Milton appeared on the screen. He was naked apart from a thick, studded black leather collar around his neck, and was crawling on all fours. He moved towards his wife.

'You know what to do,' she said in an imperious tone.

Apparently Dan knew exactly what to do. He leant forward and pressed his lips to Barbara's left shoe, kissing and licking the red leather. He gradually worked his way around the back and Barbara opened her legs so that he could put his head between them to get at the inner surfaces. She pressed her calves together, trapping his head, then relaxed the pressure so he could transfer his attention to the right foot, repeating the same process.

'Now the heels,' Barbara said.

Dan rolled on to his back. He had a strong, athletic body, with a broad and quite hairy chest, a flat belly and muscular arms and legs. His penis was already erect and Karen could see that it was strapped into some sort of leather harness that lifted and separated his balls. Barbara had raised one of her feet and poised it above her husband's mouth and he reached up and sucked enthusiastically on the narrow heel of the shoe.

For a moment Karen had an attack of conscience. It was quite obvious what had happened. The Miltons liked to videotape their obviously very kinky sex sessions. Clearly one of the tapes had been replaced in the wrong box. Karen should have turned it off and

3

chosen another tape. She even got as far as kneeling on the dark blue carpet and looking once again for the eject button on the video recorder.

'All right, now get to your feet – and do it quickly,' Barbara said sternly.

Karen hesitated. She watched as Dan scrambled to his feet, his circumcised erection bobbing up and down in front of him so violently it slapped against his belly. Of course she should have turned the video off and allowed the Miltons their privacy, but she had never seen anything like this before and it totally enthralled her. She desperately wanted to see what happened next. She stood up, took a large sip of her wine and settled back on to the sofa.

On screen Barbara was busy. She had pulled Dan's right hand up to the corner of the frame and strapped it into one of the padded leather cuffs that hung from the chains. His left hand and his ankles were treated in the same manner until he was spread-eagled across the frame, his muscular body taut and strained. Karen could see the leather harness that was wrapped around his cock more clearly now. A strap wound around the bottom of the shaft and under his balls. Attached to this were two other very thin straps that circled his balls so tightly that the skin of his scrotum was stretched taut. His cock was visibly throbbing against the restraint.

'That's better,' Barbara said. 'Are you comfortable?'

'No,' he said.

Barbara raised her hand and slapped her open palm against his cock. 'No, what?'

'No, Mistress Barbara,' Dan intoned.

'How dare you forget how to address me.'

'Sorry, Mistress Barbara.'

'Oh, you will be sorry, I can assure you of that.'

Barbara walked out of the shot. The camera was

obviously positioned on a fixed tripod to take in about two or three feet on either side of the frame, but nothing else.

A moment later she was back, carrying a riding crop with a braided leather handle and a gag. She tucked the whip under her arm then raised the gag. It consisted of an orange ball attached to a leather strap.

'Open your mouth,' Barbara instructed. 'We don't want to let the neighbours hear you scream, do we now?'

Dan opened his mouth and Barbara forced the ball into his mouth and behind his teeth, buckling the leather strap tightly around his head. The gag was so big it forced Dan's lips wide apart.

'That's better,' Barbara said, patting his distended cheek.

She walked around behind the frame, carefully examining her husband's helplessly bound body, running her satin-gloved hand down his back and over his buttocks.

'Do you agree that you need to be punished?'

Dan nodded his head.

'Then I think it's time we began, don't you?'

Barbara took the crop in her right hand, raised it to the level of her shoulder and slashed it down on to Dan's unprotected buttocks. His whole body shuddered and he cried out, the sound effectively muffled by the gag. But almost before the cry had died away Barbara raised the crop again and slashed it down twice in quick succession.

'Three nice red welts,' she said. She wrapped her arms around his chest and pressed her body into his back, rubbing her belly against his buttocks. He moaned, a noise that was a mixture of agony and ecstasy.

5

Each stroke, each concussion of leather on flesh, had had a profound effect on Karen. She felt her sex spasm sharply. Her nipples had hardened too, pressing against the soft material of her bra as though trying to bore through it.

Barbara's tongue licked her husband's ear, then pushed right inside it. 'Do you want more?' she whispered.

He shook his head violently.

'Pity,' Barbara said. 'Because you're going to get more.'

She came around the front of the frame and raised the crop. Karen could see Dan's eyes widening as he continued to shake his head. Barbara sliced the crop down on the top of his thighs, narrowly missing his cock. She aimed a second blow slightly lower.

Again Karen felt her body respond. She was wearing a light blue tracksuit, bra and panties, and realised to her surprise that she had buried her hand deep between her legs and was pressing in on it with her thighs.

'That's enough for the moment. What do you say?'

Through the gag Dan managed to produce muffled words that sounded like, 'Thank you, Mistress Barbara.'

'Good boy.'

Barbara circled his rock hard cock with her gloved hand and squeezed it until she made him moan. A drop of liquid had formed at the tip of his urethra and it dripped on to the floor. Forming a fist Barbara casually wanked her hand up and down the shaft a couple of times and Karen saw Dan's whole body tense.

'Not yet you don't,' Barbara said, letting it go. 'It'll be a long time before you're allowed any pleasure. A long time. I mightn't even bother with you tonight.' She laughed, turned her back on him and walked out of the picture. 'I'm going to get a drink. I have no idea how long I'll be. Don't go away,' she said, and Karen heard a door open then close again.

Dan stood in his bondage, unable to do anything but struggle against his chains, which he did quite violently at first. Then, realising he was getting nowhere, he resorted to pumping his hips as if trying to fuck the air.

Suddenly the screen went fuzzy. After a second or two the picture was restored. This time it showed another angle of the same grey room. The camera must have been moved around and was pointing at a flat slatted wooden frame about the size of a small double bed. Leather straps were attached to it at various points, and leather cuffs like the one on the vertical metal frame were clipped to chains at each corner. Hanging above it was a white rope that had been threaded through a pulley and tied to a cleat on the wall behind.

Barbara, in the same outfit, strode into the shot from a position that suggested it had been her who had adjusted the camera. She stood at the foot of the frame with her arms akimbo and her legs apart.

'Get over here,' she said, her tone still unyielding.

Dan crawled over to her on all fours as he had done before. Karen could see three long red stripes decorating his buttocks. He came to rest in front of his wife, his eyes level with her belly.

'Take my panties down,' she ordered.

'Yes, Mistress Barbara,' he said. He raised his hands.

'No, you fool,' she said, slapping them down. 'Use your mouth.' She reached behind his head and unstrapped the gag, letting it fall to the ground.

Dan leant forward. Awkwardly he tried to grasp the tight slippery material with his lips. It was quite clear that this was impossible so he ran his tongue along the side of the panties and pulled them out slightly so he could grasp them with his teeth. Then he began tugging them down. He managed to get the waistband over her thighs but the crotch was so deeply buried in her sex that he could not free it, however hard he tugged.

'You are completely useless,' Barbara said. She stepped away from him, pulling the panties down herself. They fell to the floor. 'Pick them up,' she said, stepping out of them.

To Karen's astonishment Barbara's sex was completely shaven. Her mons was smooth and sleek and she could see the first inch or two of her rather plump labia nestling between her legs.

Dan apparently knew better than to try and use his hands again. He stooped down and picked the red satin panties up with his teeth. Barbara stuffed them into his mouth.

'Now get on the frame,' she instructed.

Dan did as he was ordered. Barbara knelt at his side and wrapped leather cuffs around his wrists and ankles, spread-eagling him for a second time, but now horizontally. She adjusted the chains that held the cuffs until his body was stretched taut. For a moment she stood looking down at him as if admiring her work. Karen could see Dan's eyes staring at her long legs in the sheer black stockings, the black nylon welts pulled into peaks on her creamy thighs.

'My turn now,' she said.

She swung her thigh across his head so her sex was poised immediately over his mouth and she was facing his feet, then plucked the panties out of his mouth and threw them aside. Slowly she lowered herself down on to him, until her smooth but bulging labia were an inch away from his lips.

Karen watched as he raised his head and pressed his tongue into the slit of her sex. He moved it all the way up and all the way back two or three times, then concentrated on her clitoris, the tip of his tongue batting it from side to side. Barbara moaned loudly. She clutched both her breasts in her hands, her fingers tweaking at her nipples, then squirmed down on him, pressing her sex against his mouth and rolling her hips.

Dan's mouth all but disappeared underneath her, but Karen could see he was still moving, his tongue no doubt, continuing to work on her clit. After a few minutes Barbara lifted herself up off him altogether, and ran her hand down to her sex, briefly thrusting one finger then two into her vagina. The role she had been playing, the way she had reduced her husband to her slave, had clearly excited her since Dan's face was glistening under the rather harsh lights, her juices running all over it.

Barbara moaned again as she buried her fingers deep in her own body, her big breasts quivering. Then she withdrew them and lowered herself, once more grinding down on Dan's mouth.

In seconds she was coming. She pinched her nipples between the finger and thumb of both hands and lifted her breasts, straining the buttery flesh up out of the support of the basque. This made her moan even louder, partly in pain. But she did not let go. As Dan's tongue worked ceaselessly on her clit, she shuddered, threw her head back, opened her mouth and let out a long, low scream.

As Karen watched she felt her own body throbbing too. Quite unconsciously she had worked her finger against her clit, pressing the tracksuit and the panties she was wearing underneath into her sex. She had never seen anything like this in her life, but however bizarre and outré there was no doubt that it was exciting her in

9

a way that nothing else ever had. She could feel her juices running down the inside of her vagina and her nipples were so hard they felt like little pebbles.

Barbara lifted herself off her husband. She picked the red satin panties off the frame and wiped his face with them, then stuffed them into his mouth. Swinging round to face him, she straddled his chest, then 'walked' back until her sex was directly over his erection. In this position, with her legs spread apart, Karen could see every detail, from the perfectly round and puckered circle of her anus to the long open crack of her sex. Barbara's outer labia were thick and rubbery while the inner lips, pursed around the entrance to her vagina, were thin and delicate. She thought she could even see her clitoris, a little pink button just under the fourchette. It looked swollen and engorged.

Of course Karen had seen naked girls in the showers at school but she had never seen an adult woman so lewdly exposed, and once again she felt her clit spasm wildly. She would not have imagined that the sight could have such a profound effect on her, but what she was seeing made her feel a unique pulse of excitement, like nothing she had felt before.

Barbara grasped her husband's cock in her hand and guided it into her labia. Using it like a dildo she brushed the top of the glans back and forth across her clit, making herself moan. She teased herself like this for a few minutes then pushed his cock to the entrance of her vagina and held it there.

'You are not allowed to come. If you come without my permission you will not be allowed to come again for a whole week. You do understand that, don't you?'

'Yes, Mistress Barbara,' Dan said, his voice muffled by the panties, though Karen could see his cock was already spasming between Barbara's fingers.

10

'Good.'

Barbara dropped her full weight on him, forcing his cock into the depths of her sex. She moaned loudly then ground herself down on him, wriggling her hips from side to side. Then she began riding him. There was no question of subtlety or finesse; she rode him wildly, pulling herself almost off him then slamming herself back down again, each penetration making her moan with pleasure.

Karen could actually see his cock sliding in and out of her, slick with her juices, the cock strap at its base cutting deeply into the tumescent flesh. The strange thing was that every forward thrust produced a feeling deep in Karen's sex, almost as if the cock was plunging into her.

Barbara slowed her rhythm, almost stopping. She drew herself up off Dan until most of his glans was visible, then dropped down on him so he was buried completely in her. But this time she did not lift herself again. Instead she screwed herself down, spreading her legs further apart as if wanting to gain an extra inch of penetration, her clit crushed between their bodies. Then she let out a piercing scream and her whole body shuddered.

Karen took off her tracksuit bottoms and pulled the crotch of her little white cotton panties aside. With about as much subtlety as Barbara had displayed she jammed two fingers into her vagina. It was soaking wet.

On screen Barbara lifted herself off her husband, Dan's cock slipping out of her body and slapping down against his belly. She got to her feet.

'Perhaps I should leave you here to cool off,' she said. She reached forward and plucked the panties from his mouth.

'No, please Mistress,' he said.

'What do you want then?' she asked.

Dan did not reply. He strained his body up towards his wife and bucked his hips.

She laughed. 'You don't imagine I'm really going to let you fuck me do you?'

One of her stockings had wrinkled at the knee and she put her foot up on the frame near his head and stooped to straighten it, using both her hands to smooth the nylon from ankle to thigh. She undid one of the suspenders then clipped it back into the darker welt of the stocking so it was held perfectly tight. Karen could see Dan's eyes following every movement, his cock twitching in its harness.

Without a word Barbara disappeared out of shot. She was back only seconds later carrying an odd-looking device. It seemed to consist of a cylindrical dildo crudely moulded to resemble an erect male penis, except that at the top and bottom leather straps projected from each side.

'No,' Dan said when he saw it.

'No? You would rather I left you here in that state?' She nodded at his cock.

'Please don't use that,' he said.

'You don't have any choice,' she said testily.

She knelt on the wooden frame, pulled his cock into a vertical position and placed the cylinder against it. Then she wound the lower strap around his already tightly strapped cock and buckled it into position. The upper strap fitted just under the ridge at the base of his glans. She stood up.

'Don't you think it's good of me to give you this privilege?' she said. 'What do you say?'

'Thank you, Mistress Barbara,' he said, clearly afraid that any further show of petulance would bring him worse treatment.

Barbara straddled his chest, facing his feet, giving him a view of her smooth, hairless sex. She fiddled with the base of the dildo and it began to hum. Karen saw Dan's cock twitch wildly, springing up from his belly before bouncing down again.

'I give you permission to come,' Barbara said. She wriggled herself back towards his face then pinched both of his nipples with her long fingernails and pulled them up.

Dan moaned loudly. His cock jerked up off his belly again three or four times, then Karen saw a jet of spunk shoot from its tip, arcing up over his body so far that some of it spattered against Barbara's belly, though most landed on his chest.

'Good boy,' she said.

The picture went fuzzy again, then the screen turned a uniform blue. The video was over.

Karen was almost unaware of it. The images from the screen had burned themselves into her mind so deeply that she only had to close her eyes to see them again, to see Barbara's shaven sex poised above Dan's cock, to watch his spunk jetting from his wildly throbbing cock. She thrust her fingers deeper into her body and used her thumb to rub against her clit. In seconds, in less than seconds, she was coming, every nerve in her body set on edge, her sex contracting around her fingers while her clit spasmed furiously. She screamed, a scream as fervent as the one Barbara had given on the tape, and her whole body seemed to go rigid, the hardness of her muscle in stark contrast to the melting softness at the centre of her sex. She had never felt anything like this before.

It took her a few minutes to recover. Her orgasm had been so powerful that it was almost like waking from a deep sleep and trying to remember where you were.

She opened her eyes and gazed at the television, unable to recall for a second why she was there and what she had been doing. Then it all came flooding back.

She got to her feet a little shakily, picked up and finished her glass of wine, then ejected the tape from the video recorder and placed it back in the *Love Story* box. All the videos were stored in a large cabinet with black glass doors but now she noticed that as well as the many official tapes there were literally dozens of other tapes, numbered but not titled with a felt pen. Very determinedly she avoided the temptation to get one out.

Karen felt a wave of embarrassment at having witnessed what was clearly a very private moment. She had read magazine articles about couples who used sado-masochism and bondage as a way of spicing up their sex lives but she had never come across it in real life. In the weeks that she had lived with them neither Barbara nor Dan had given any hint that these were the sort of sex games they obviously enjoyed. Although now she came to think of it, she had caught Barbara being rather domineering to her husband on a couple of occasions but she had put that down to normal marital interplay. She had had no idea that, in the bedroom, he was prepared to be her total slave, or that Barbara clearly relished the idea of being his absolute master.

Her own reaction to what she had seen was just as unequivocal. She was not a virgin but she had to admit to herself that her sexual experiences so far had been less than satisfactory. The three lovers she had had to date had all been conscientious and accomplished, but her reaction to them, to the feeling of their erections thrusting into her body, had been muted. The sensations had been pleasant enough but none of the men

14

had brought her to a climax, and certainly none of them had ever given her the sort of pleasure she had felt a few minutes ago by her own hand.

And that in itself was puzzling. She had masturbated before but it too had proved a far from satisfactory experience. Occasionally, usually when she was in bed at night and unable to sleep, she had stroked her clitoris, slipped one or two fingers into her vagina, and brought herself to a pleasant crescendo which she had thought of as an orgasm. But again it was nothing in comparison to this roaring flood of feelings.

What was more, her body refused to relax; though her orgasm had been all-consuming it had left her wanting more. She could still feel little tremors of pleasure pulsing through her sex, and her clitoris was so swollen it seemed to be thrusting out between her labia. Her breasts felt heavy and she was intensely aware of her nipples. The impulse to collapse back on the sofa and masturbate again was, she thought, the strongest sexual need she had ever encountered. But she resisted it. The night, she told herself firmly, was young. Her imagination was running riot. There were all sorts of things she wanted to do before the Miltons got back.

She poured herself another glass of wine and climbed the stairs, letting herself into the Miltons' bedroom. She felt like a thief in the night but her curiosity had got the better of her. The bedroom had a large built-in wardrobe that occupied one whole wall of the room. She opened the sliding doors on one side and found a rack of male clothes. The middle section was hung with Barbara's dresses and the other end was fitted with shelves and drawers containing Dan's socks and pants and what looked like Barbara's lingerie – everyday wear, functional bras and panties in cotton and polyester. There was also a drawer of more alluring items in silk and satin and lace, but they were mostly teddies and bodies and bra and pants sets. A third drawer contained packets of tights, divided into their different colours.

They were not what Karen was looking for. There were two largish chests of drawers on either side of the big double bed. Guessing from the bowl of rings and trinkets on the right-hand chest that this was Barbara's side of the bed, she opened the top drawer.

She found herself staring at a selection of dildoes. There were four or five at least, all in different shapes and materials, from one the size of a finger in cream plastic to a black rubber example, crudely fashioned to resemble a male phallus, and so big that Karen could not imagine how any woman could accommodate it. There were other items too, a thick metal chain with two odd-looking oval clips at each end, a thin thread with two adjustable loops, and a pair of metal handcuffs, a blindfold, a gag and two blue jars of what looked like cold cream.

Karen opened the next drawer down. She felt a thrill of pleasure as she fingered through the contents. She had found what she was looking for. There were five basques, including the red satin one she had just seen on video. There was one in black leather and a dramatic violet-coloured one in soft velvet. There were two in PVC that laced up the front, one black and one red, as well as waspies and suspender belts, platform bras and bras with no cups at all, just an arrangement of straps that surrounded the breasts.

She opened the bottom drawer. It contained a huge selection of stockings in an amazing variety of colours, some sheer, some opaque, some patterned. There were white and black fishnets, lacy-topped hold-ups in glossy black, and stockings with fully fashioned heels and a seam.

Carefully trying to remember exactly how the drawer had looked so she could put it back that way later, Karen extracted the red satin basque. She held it up in front of her. Though Barbara was fifteen years older than her they both had remarkably similar figures, tall and slender, and, as Karen had seen so graphically for herself, with roughly the same size bust.

Karen dropped the basque on the big double bed and stripped off her tracksuit top, bra and sodden wet panties. She checked her watch again to make sure there was absolutely no possibility of being disturbed unexpectedly. Even if the Miltons did not stay to dance and left immediately after the dinner, they would not be home for at least two hours, and it was more likely they wouldn't be home until two or three in the morning. She had plenty of time.

Quickly, she wrapped the basque around her body. It felt cold to the touch and made her shiver. But it was a shiver of pure pleasure. As she fastened it at the back and the garment tightened around her body, the boned corset reduced her waist to almost hourglass proportions, making her catch her breath.

There was a mirror on the wall opposite the foot of the bed and she stared at her reflection looking for any changes. Karen had long blonde hair that fell to her shoulders and a delicately featured face, with a small mouth, pouting lips, a straight nose and high hollow cheeks. Her big blue eyes stared back at her with an expression of feigned innocence, a smile hovering on her lips.

The crescent-shaped cups of the bra lifted her round, firm breasts and exposed them, making them feel prickly and sensitive. Her nipples, a dark ruby red, had puckered into tight knots.

She went back to the chest of drawers and pulled out a pair of black glossy stockings like the ones she had seen in the video. Being extra careful not to ladder them she pulled them up her legs and clipped them into the suspenders that dangled from the basque. She had never worn stockings before and they created a strange sensation. The skin above the welts felt incredibly soft and vulnerable in contrast to the tight nylon below. The suspenders were tight and bit into the pliant flesh of her hips and thighs.

There was one thing missing. The shoes. Karen searched the wardrobe and soon found seven pairs with the ultra-high heels. There were two pairs of ankle boots, two pairs of black suede shoes, with one each in red and black patent leather. The final pair were PVC thigh-high boots. Wanting to exactly mimic the video she had just seen Karen eased her feet into the red patent leather. Barbara was probably one size bigger than her but they fitted perfectly well.

Karen turned and looked into the mirror again; she hardly recognised herself. The tight basque, the stockings and the shoes had transformed her body. Her breasts and the band of flesh between the top of the stockings and the bottom of the basque looked yielding and impossibly creamy in contrast to the shiny red satin. The shoes had shaped her legs, and as she turned to look over her shoulder to glimpse her back she could see that her buttocks were pouted and firm, the gluteal fold deeper than it had ever been before. She looked like an expensive whore.

The sight made her sex throb strongly. She would have liked to find the gloves and the satin panties to complete the picture but she could not wait. She lay on the bed

18

without pulling back the cream-coloured counterpane and opened her legs, staring at the view of her sex in the mirror. She could not see as much of her vulva as she had seen of Barbara's early on because her sex was covered with a thick bush of fair pubic hair. But as she bent her knees, digging the heels of the shoes into the bedding, and spreading her thighs even further apart, she saw the mouth of her vagina wink open. The scarlet maw glistened and she could feel her juices running down the velvet walls of her vagina and out over her labia.

Lifting her buttocks she moved her hand under her legs and jammed her fingers into her sex. It had never felt so hot or so raw, all her nerves reacting with a huge pulse of feeling. But even with three fingers thrust in right up to the knuckle it was not enough. She wanted more and she knew exactly where to get it.

The clothes made her look like a whore but they also made her *feel* like a different person too and that emboldened her. Pulling her fingers from her sex, she stretched across to the bedside chest, opened the top drawer again and extracted a gold torpedo-shaped dildo. Smiling at herself in the mirror she licked the phallic object, then sucked it into her mouth. It was a measure of her sexual ingenuousness that she had never used a dildo before. She had seen them in the windows of sex shops since she had arrived in London but had never given them a second thought. As her body had been so slow to respond sexually in the past she had come to think of herself as having a very low sex drive, and therefore had little interest or curiosity in any aspect of the subject.

Her clit pulsed strongly as if demanding her attention. She scissored her legs apart and turned the gnarled base at the bottom of the cylinder. The dildo began to hum loudly.

On another occasion she could imagine teasing herself with this instrument, running the tip over her breasts or along her thigh. But tonight the shock of what she had discovered and the effect it had had on her left her in no mood for subtleties, and she jammed the vibrator right up against her clit. Almost immediately her body responded with a huge wave of pleasure. The vibrations rippled out from her clit until they reached the depths of her vagina where a new set of nerves began oscillating at the same frequency.

This was wonderful. In seconds she was on the brink of orgasm. Her eyes were forced closed and there in the darkness the images of the video waited for her again. She saw Barbara's satin-gloved hand guiding Dan's cock into her shiny wet labia. She imagined herself doing the same thing, feeling his heat and hardness right there, teasing him with her body while he was completely powerless to do anything about it. She saw his body stretched out across the frame, bound and helpless, completely at her mercy.

Karen arched her head back until it was almost at right angles to her spine and opened her mouth to scream with delight, but her second orgasm was so intense that no sound came out.

She couldn't believe how quickly she had come. What had passed for orgasms when she'd masturbated before had always taken so long to achieve. This one had been virtually instantaneous.

And once again it had left her wanting more. The moment the wave of pleasure subsided she pushed the tip of the vibrating dildo lower, until it was nestled in her labia. She raised her head to look in the mirror and could see the gold shaft glinting in the light.

This time she did tease herself. She eased the vibrating tip of the dildo into her vagina an inch or two then pulled it out again. She stroked it up and down the whole length of her slit, brushing her clit and causing a new frisson of excitement, before bringing it back to her vagina. She angled it inward again, and then suddenly, tired of that game, thrust it inside. Her sex was so wet there was no resistance and the dildo plunged right up to the neck of her womb. Her sex clenched around it strongly, producing a sharp pulse of pleasure that made her moan. The vibrations immediately charged through the nerves deep inside her, nerves that she had hardly been aware of before. Obviously determined to assert their new-found dynamism they reacted with waves of sheer ecstacy.

Karen withdrew her hand from the base of the vibrator and tried to hold it in place with the muscles of her sex. She could see it in the mirror, her labia pursed around the gold shaft. But her muscles were too weak or her sex too slippery, as the dildo began sliding out. Quickly she pushed it back up with her finger.

She was coming again now. In the mirror she could see the tight red satin that banded her body and the taut suspenders that held the stockings. She had never worn clothes like this before but there was no doubt in her mind that they were adding to her excitement, not only by fuelling her fantasies but physically too; the constriction of the corset seemed to increase the intensity of everything she felt, like a lid screwed on a pressure cooker. Her whole body was trembling as she allowed the dildo to slide a few inches out of her vagina then jammed it up again. As the tip of the hard plastic hit the neck of her womb an explosion of feeling overtook her. Her clitoris went into spasm and now she did scream, long and loud, a crescendo of sound that exactly matched the soaring pleasure she was feeling.

She lay on the bed, finally sated. Releasing her grip on the dildo she felt it slowly slide from her body. As it finally fell on to the bed another tremor of pleasure made her gasp.

For a while she could do nothing but lay there staring up at the ceiling, her eyes glazed, as if she were floating, her mind on another plane. Only slowly did reality seep back and she realised that she had to get up.

Quickly she stripped off the shoes, stockings and basque, replacing them exactly where she had found them. She wiped the dildo on the top of her tracksuit – not wishing to do it on one of the bathroom towels in case it was noticed – and replaced that too. She straightened the counterpane. There was a slight wet patch in the middle of it but she was sure that would dry by the time the Miltons got home. She collected her tracksuit bottoms from the front room then went to bed, feeling totally exhausted. It had certainly not been the night she had planned for herself.

Chapter Two

KAREN SAT DOWN at her desk in a daze. It was a twenty-minute busride from the Miltons house in Brook Green to the Angels offices in Holland Park, but this morning she could barely remember the journey at all. Her mind was elsewhere.

Karen's ambition had always been to work in the City. She saw herself as a trader or a stockbroker, and had worked in Christchurch as a secretary in an accountant's office, imagining that would be good experience. But after receiving a number of rejections from City firms for their trainee programmes she had decided she needed to move up to London so she would be closer to the action and be available for interviews more easily.

After two weeks of trudging the streets of the city, however, she had found nothing that was even vaguely suitable and was rapidly running out of money. She had needed a job, any job, and had seen an advert for Angels in the *Evening Standard*. It was an agency that solved household problems, finding decorators, cleaners, nannies, housekeepers or cooks for busy professionals. She had gone along for an interview with at least twenty other candidates and had been offered the job on the spot.

Angels had spacious offices and employed ten girls to man the telephones to answer incoming calls. They were backed up by five researchers who found the people who would be used to solve the problems, then took up their references and did everything they could to establish that the standard of service they promised was the one they would deliver.

'Looks like you had a rough night,' Tina said, as she passed Karen's desk on the way to her own.

'Something like that,' Karen said.

'Lucky you.'

Tina had shown Karen the ropes when she'd first arrived and they had been good friends ever since, though their personalities were completely different. Where Karen thought of herself as shy, reserved and introverted, Tina was gregarious, forthright and never afraid to call a spade a spade. She appeared to have an endless stream of men on tap, which was not surprising as she was terribly pretty. She had curly blonde hair, and though she was short she was slender and shapely and liked to wear what Karen considered quite provocative clothes. This morning for instance she was wearing a pink mini-skirt over a skin-tight white body with a plunging neckline that revealed her consider-able cleavage.

'You had a coffee yet?'

Karen shook her head.

'I'll get them.'

As she watched Tina head toward the little kitchen area at the back of the office the phone rang on her desk. She answered it and dealt with a query regarding the cleaners she had arranged for one of her clients.

By the time she had finished Tina was back with two mugs of coffee. She sat in the chrome and leather chair at the side of Karen's desk.

'So are you going to tell me about it?' she said. 'Who was he? I thought you were seeing Roger. He didn't seem all that exciting.'

Karen was feeling guilty and embarrassed about what had happened. She had had no right to invade the Miltons' privacy in the way she had done, and even less to put on Barbara's clothes and use her dildo. She found herself blushing at the thought.

'You're blushing!' Tina said. 'It must have been hot.'

'I think I'm regretting what happened.'

'Did you enjoy it?'

'Yes.' There was no doubt about that.

'Then what's there to regret? As long as you had a good time and no one got hurt that's all that matters isn't it?'

'I suppose so.'

She would have liked to tell Tina the whole truth but she wasn't ready for that yet. She had had a largely sleepless night, tossing and turning, with images of Barbara and Dan, and of herself in the mirror in their bedroom, whirling around in her head as she tried to understand what had made her respond so dramatically. The only conclusion she had been able to come up with was an uncomfortable one; that what had turned her on so markedly was not the fact that she had watched a video of two people having sex, but the sort of sex they were having. Lying on their bed with the dildo crammed into her body it was the thought of Dan bound and powerless that had turned her on most.

'And what about you, what did you get up to last night?' she said, trying to change the subject.

'The Rt Hon. Mortimer Bladstock.'

'Who's he?'

'I've no idea but he's got a big Bentley and a whole

house around the corner from here. Unfortunately for me he also had a tiny dick.' She held up her little finger and laughed. 'So the endless quest for Mr Right goes on.'

The phone rang again.

'See you later,' she said, taking her coffee back to her own desk.

A few minutes later, as she finished with the second query of the day, Malcolm Travers walked in. Malcolm was the head of the agency and one of the most attractive men Karen had ever seen. He had thick curly black hair, a very symmetrical face with a straight nose, large dark brown eyes and a firm, jutting chin. He was tall and slender and moved with the grace of a man who was comfortable with his body. She knew he belonged to the local gym, and suspected that under the impeccably tailored suits he always wore was a fit and well-toned body.

'Morning, Karen,' he said, as he walked past her desk. 'Are you settling in all right?'

'Fine thanks, Mr Travers, I mean Malcolm.' He had told her he preferred the staff to call him by his Christian name.

'Good. I have heard good reports about you.' He smiled, revealing his regular and very white teeth, then climbed the spiral staircase to the first floor which was a gallery at the back of the room, his office overlooking most of the front part of the ground floor.

The time passed quickly. Angels was busy and a local mail shot had produced a new wave of customers. When the phone on Karen's desk rang again it was at least the twentieth call that morning.

'Hello, Karen Masters, how may I help you?'

'Karen, it's Pamela.'

'Hi Pamela, how are you?'

'Well, largely thanks to you I'm fine.'

Pamela Stern had been one of Karen's first clients. In fact she was a friend of Malcolm's and he had given her to Karen to deal with, she suspected, as a test. Pamela had just moved into a new house and had wanted a decorator and a carpenter. Though she refused to explain to Karen exactly what was involved she had said the work was a little unusual and required someone who was not easily shocked. The researchers had found a man who could do both jobs, and as he had not complained about whatever Pamela had in mind, he had obviously been unshockable.

'Did our man work out?'

'He was perfect. Very discreet.'

That was a strange word, Karen thought. 'Good, I'm glad.'

'The thing is, I wondered if you were doing anything tomorrow night. I'd like to invite you around for dinner as a way of thanking you.'

'It's really not necessary.'

'I know it's not. But I would like it. Would you?'

Karen had nothing else on. Her starting salary was low and she had nothing left over for nights on the town, so had to spend most of her evenings at home. A night out would make a change. Besides, she was terribly curious to know what Pamela's special requirements had involved.

'All right, I'll be there. What time?'

'Say eight.'

'Fine.'

'You've got the address haven't you?'

'That's where I have to send the bill,' Karen said.

'Bring it with you, I'll give you a cheque.' She ended the call.

Pamela had come into the office one day and Karen

remembered her well. About ten years older than her she was a strikingly beautiful woman, with flaming red hair that surrounded her face in soft waves. She was extremely tall, Karen estimated well over six feet, and though it would not have been fair to describe her as fat, she was certainly large, with an impressive chest, and large limbs to match. But there was something about her attitude to life and the sparkle in her eyes that Karen had found beguiling, and she was really glad of the opportunity to get to know her better.

She didn't have much time to think of anything else for the rest of the day, and ate her lunch at her desk, dealing with new calls. It was only when she got on the bus to go home that she found herself thinking about Barbara and Dan again. She had only seen them very briefly this morning as she'd been late for work, and wasn't at all sure how she was going to react that evening over the meal they generally shared. It would be difficult not to overlay the image of Barbara wielding the riding crop on the real one of her standing in the kitchen, just as it would be impossible to see Dan without remembering how he had looked tied to the frame with his cock bound by a leather harness. She would have to try. She certainly had no intention of even hinting that she knew their secret.

Letting herself into the house she saw that Barbara was sitting in the front room with a glass of wine in her hand. It was pretty obvious that she was troubled about something.

'Hi, sweetie,' she said. 'Do you fancy a drink?'

Karen fancied a drink very much. She walked into the room and sat down opposite Barbara, as she poured a glass of white wine.

'Cheers,' Barbara said.

'Cheers,' Karen repeated, raising her glass.

'Look,' she said. 'I think we've got an apology to make to you.'

Karen swallowed hard, not knowing what to expect. 'An apology?'

'Yes. I saw the tape you had out last night, *Love Story*?'

'Yes.' Karen couldn't stop herself from blushing.

'It wasn't *Love Story* was it? I was sorting through the tapes this afternoon. I must have put the wrong tape in the wrong box. I'm really sorry, I don't know how it happened. We were just careless I guess. We'd been watching them in bed over the weekend and I suddenly remembered in the middle of dinner last night that I'd put one of them back in that box. I'm really sorry. It must have been terribly embarrassing for you. It won't happen again I promise you. I'm going to lock them all away.'

'There's no need to apologise, really. I didn't mind. When I realized . . .'

'Did you watch much of it?'

Karen couldn't lie. 'Yes, I'm afraid I did.'

'And were you shocked?'

Karen sipped the wine, pausing before she replied, 'Do you want the truth?' She had no intention of telling her the whole truth.

'If you don't mind telling me.'

'The truth is I was totally fascinated. I'd never seen anything like that before. You looked so beautiful, so sexy. It made me feel sexy. I loved what you were wearing. I've never worn stockings, and those high heels . . .' It all came pouring out. Much more than she had intended to say.

'It turned you on didn't it? For God's sake don't tell your mother.'

29

'I wasn't planning too. How long have you been . . .'

'A dominatrix? Oh, long before I met Dan. I never got much pleasure from ordinary sex. Do you want to know the whole story?'

'I told you, I think it's fascinating.'

'Well, I suppose it was about ten years ago when I was twenty-five. I'd been to bed with my fair share of men but I can't say I'd ever really enjoyed sex. Then I met this man called Peter. He was very rich. Loaded actually. I went out with him a couple of times but he never so much as kissed me. I was beginning to think he was gay. Then he finally asked me back to his house. He appeared terribly shy and ill at ease so I asked him what was the matter. He said he thought I was gorgeous, that he fancied me madly but that he found it very difficult to have ordinary sex. I was intrigued. I asked him what he meant and he told me that if I really wanted to know he'd better show me, but that he'd quite understand if I never wanted anything to do with him again. He even gave me my cab fare home. Then he told me to give him fifteen minutes and pointed to a door at the end of the hall.' Barbara picked up her wine and sipped it. 'So that's what I did. After the time was up I opened the door. The room was completely black. It had all sorts of odd-looking pieces of equipment, like frames and chains and pulleys. He had stripped all his clothes off and was spread over a sort of vaulting horse. He'd strapped his ankles into cuffs on one side of it, and was stretching over it with a rubber hood over his face. Next to him was a riding crop. It was pretty obvious what he wanted me to do.'

'And did you?'

'It was extraordinary, Karen. I had never felt so turned on in my life. I can still remember it so well. My pulse was racing and my sex was throbbing so much I thought I was going to come right there on the spot. I'm not being too crude am I?'

'No.'

'Well, I walked around the front of the horse thing and saw there were cuffs at the other side too. So I bent down and buckled his wrists into them so he was completely helpless, then picked up the crop . . .'

'That was the first time?'

'Yes. It was wonderful. I felt completely in control. It was what had obviously been missing in my life. The next day I went out and bought all the books I could find about sado-masochism and submission and domination. I had no idea it was such a big thing.'

'Is it?'

'Oh yes. There are men who can only get real sexual pleasure from being totally submissive, and women who only get it if they are totally in control, and vice versa of course. Some women like to be on the submissive side.' This idea clearly did not appeal to her as Karen saw her shudder.

'And Dan?'

'Dan is a submissive. He has a very responsible job. I think that's part of it. He gives orders all day long so at night he likes to flip the coin. He does exactly what I tell him to do.'

'And that excites you?'

'I think you've seen that for yourself haven't you?'

Karen blushed as she nodded.

'So now you know all our secrets.'

'I had no idea,' Karen said.

'No one knows what goes on behind closed doors do they?'

Karen felt a sense of relief. Now that it was all out in the open it seemed much less important and was easier

31

to cope with. What Barbara and Dan did for their sexual gratification was none of her business. Of course she still had to work out her own reaction to what she had seen, but perhaps she would be able to forget about it, particularly if Barbara removed temptation by locking the tapes away. Was out of sight really out of mind?

The tall, narrow house was in a street off Holland Park Avenue. There was no front garden and the door opened directly on to the pavement. Karen pressed the little illuminated bell on the doorjamb and heard it ring inside.

'Good evening, Madam.'

The door was opened by a woman with long blonde hair wearing a traditional black maid's dress and white lace apron. She was quite pretty, with heavily made-up eyes and thick pancake make-up on her face, her shapely legs sheathed in black fishnet.

'Ms Stern?' Karen said.

'Yes, please come in. Ms Stern is in the sitting room.' The maid had a low, gruff voice. She ushered Karen inside and closed the door. 'May I take your coat?'

The maid helped Karen out of the lightweight mac she was wearing then led her along a narrow corridor to the back of the house. The corridor had a wooden floor and was painted white with a huge collection of pictures all along one wall, their frames so close together they were touching. Karen glanced at one or two briefly. Some were photographs, others were prints and watercolours, and there were also some oils, but they all shared the same theme: the naked or semi-naked human body. Karen glimpsed a photograph of a heavy, swollen breast, an oil of a black suspender clipping into a lacy white stocking top, and a pen and ink drawing of a large erect penis about to penetrate the outline of an equally exaggerated vulva.

'Karen, how are you?'

Pamela Stern got to her feet, came over to Karen and kissed her on both cheeks. She was wearing a black silk catsuit, the material so tight it fitted her like a second skin, cutting deeply into the groove between her legs, the deep V-neck revealing quite a lot of her large breasts. Her black patent leather ankle boots had the sort of heel Karen had only seen before on the similar examples in Barbara's wardrobe. They increased her considerable height still further.

'This is beautiful,' Karen said, gazing admiringly round her.

The room was decorated in shades of oatmeal and cream, with walls panelled in obviously old reclaimed oak. The wooden floor extended into the sitting room where it had been dotted with some Kelim rugs. The furniture was a combination of ultra-modern and antique, with a huge white sofa and an ornate French walnut cabinet in one corner.

'Sit down, please. Would you like a glass of champagne?'

'How lovely.'

There was a modern glass coffee table in front of the sofa. On the top of it was a silver wine cooler holding a bottle of Taittinger *Blanc de Blanc* champagne, swathed in ice, and two thin champagne flutes, one of which already held champagne.

Pamela filled the second glass and handed it to Karen.

'Bottoms up,' Pamela said, clinking their glasses together. 'Sit down, make yourself comfortable. I thought we might eat on the terrace but it looks like it's going to be too cold.'

There was a French window leading from the sitting room on to a small terrace, decked with shrubs and flowers. But the early summer weather had turned cold, with a bitter east wind, and it looked as if it might rain.

The maid stood in the doorway. 'Will there be anything else, Madam?' she asked.

'Not at the moment,' Pamela replied in a rather unfriendly tone. 'But don't go wandering off.'

'No Madam.' The maid disappeared leaving the sitting room door open.

'Well, your decorator did a good job don't you think?'

'It's marvellous.'

'All in two weeks.'

Karen sipped the champagne. It was creamy and delicious. 'I was a little puzzled by your requirements.'

'Your man was exactly right. In fact I think he'd done it before. He was a very good carpenter as well. Come on, let's eat. I'm starving.'

They took the champagne through into the dining room at the front of the house and dined off pâté, cold salmon and salad, and raspberry pavlova, all served by the maid. They drank the bottle of champagne and a fruity Chablis *Grande Cru*, and talked of clothes, fashion, politics and the cinema. Pamela seemed to have seen every film on current release and told Karen which to avoid.

'Would you like coffee?' she asked, at the end of the meal.

'Yes. I'm feeling very mellow,' Karen said. It was a pleasantly euphoric feeling however, and she found Pamela the most relaxing company. She was also, she thought, one of the most attractive women she had ever seen and found it difficult to avoid staring at her, her deep green eyes and high cheek bones giving her face a

34

rather haughty, aristocratic look. During the dinner Karen had also found it hard to take her eyes off the deep shadowy cleavage that the catsuit presented, the way Pamela's bosom moved as she talked, the soft pillows of flesh butting against each other, endlessly fascinating.

'Good. That was the idea. Let's take coffee in the sitting room.'

They walked back to the other room. Karen dropped into one corner of the big white sofa, kicked off her shoes and curled her legs up under her. 'You don't mind, do you?'

'Make yourself comfortable,' Pamela said. 'Would you like a brandy? I've got a really nice Camus.'

'Whatever you're having.' Karen knew she shouldn't really have anything else to drink but she was having such a good time she didn't want to hold back.

Pamela opened the walnut cabinet. It was full of every conceivable sort of drink together with a selection of lead crystal glasses. She poured brandy from a bulbous bottle into two balloon glasses and brought them over to the sofa. She handed Karen one then sat beside her.

The maid brought in a silver tray with a large silver coffee pot and tiny white porcelain demi-tasse cups. There was a plate of delicious-looking petit-fours.

'Can I ask you something?' Karen said, as the maid left. The wine had loosened her tongue.

'Anything.'

'When you first asked me for a decorator, you said it had to be someone who was not easily shocked.'

'Yes, I remember.'

'Why was that?'

Pamela laughed. 'How old are you Karen? Do you mind me asking?'

'No. I'm twenty.'

'And you've only just moved to London, is that right?'

'Yes, but I don't see—'

'And would you say *you* are easily shocked?'

'No, I don't think so.' What she had so recently discovered about Barbara and Dan had surprised her, certainly, but she couldn't say she had been shocked by it.

'All right then. I needed someone unshockable because I wanted him to do some rather special work. Have you heard of a dominatrix?'

Karen felt her cheeks glowing red. That was the way Barbara had described herself last night. 'Yes.'

'Well, that's what I do.'

'Do?'

'Men employ me to dominate them, to make them my slave.'

'I had no idea.'

'That's why I moved to this house. I needed bigger premises. My old place was too small and it was difficult in a block of flats with men coming and going. Here I've got my own front door and enough space to have a separate treatment room.'

'Treatment room?'

'Some of my dominatrix friends call theirs a dungeon but that's a bit too baroque for my taste.'

Karen was having visions of the grey room she'd seen in the video, with the metal frame and all the cuffs and chains.

'Now I understand,' she said, trying to sound calmer than she felt.

'And you're not shocked.'

'Not at all. Actually, a friend of mine . . .' Karen wasn't sure how to phrase it. 'Some friends of mine are into the same thing.'

'Really?'

'Yes. They've got a . . . a treatment room of their own.'

'So you know all about it?'

'Not all. To tell you the truth, until recently I've never been that interested in sex. I mean, I couldn't see what the fuss was about.'

Pamela was looking straight into her eyes. 'Why was that?'

'I don't know.' She sipped the brandy. 'I was never very good at having orgasms.' She would never normally have said anything so intimate to a perfect stranger but the alcohol had lowered her inhibitions.

'Past tense,' Pamela said sharply.

'Yes. When I found out what my friends were doing I got very turned on. It was extraordinary, I'd never had a feeling like it.' Karen was actually glad to be able to share her recent experiences with somebody.

'Is that so strange?'

'I think so.'

'Well I don't. You see, a lot of women think that sex is like eating or going to sleep, just another bodily function. They never give much thought to it and often don't get much out of it either. But the truth is there are many different types of sex, all kinds of sexual behaviour, and different things suit different people. Your friend is obviously like me. I like to dominate men. That's how I get my sexual satisfaction.'

'But you get paid for it.'

'I didn't in the beginning. I was lucky enough to discover that there was a huge demand for what I liked to do. That's when I decided to go into business. But it's not something I do cynically to please men. I do it to please myself, that's what I mean. If a woman really wants to enjoy sex she's got to pay attention to what her body is telling her. It might be that they get the ultimate pleasure in the missionary position; it might be something else entirely. There's no such thing as normal. Everyone is different. The point is that if you're really going to enjoy and get into sex you have to find out what you need, what your sexual nature is.'

'Nature?'

'Your sexual character, what really turns you on . . .'

That made sense to Karen. There was no denying the effect the tape and Barbara's, tight constricting corset had had on her. If Pamela was right perhaps she had inclinations to being dominant with men. She hadn't liked to think about that possibility because it implied that she was kinky and abnormal in some way, but Pamela and Barbara were both intelligent, attractive women who she liked and admired and they had no problem dealing with their special sexuality so perhaps it was not that bad after all. She finished the brandy.

'I think . . .' she began slowly. 'I think that's what may have happened to me. Discovering my sexual nature I mean. They'd made a tape of one of their sessions. I saw it by accident. But watching it really affected me.'

'There's nothing wrong with that Karen, really. It's not a disease. Shall we try a little experiment?'

'What sort of experiment?'

'Josephine, get in here immediately,' Pamela shouted imperiously.

The maid walked into the room with her head bowed.

'I am particularly unimpressed by your attitude this evening,' Pamela said. 'You've been sloppy and slap-dash haven't you?'

'Yes, Miss Pamela,' she replied, her eyes cast to the floor.

'And what do you think I should do about it?'

'Punish me, Miss Pamela.'

Karen felt her mouth drop open in astonishment.

'Oh don't worry, I fully intended to do just that,' Pamela said coolly. 'But first I want you to show my friend Karen here what a good job you can do on my shoes.'

'Yes, Mistress.'

Without the slightest hesitation Josephine dropped to her knees in front of Pamela, who was sitting with her legs crossed, one foot dangling in the air and one on the floor. The maid leant forward and began licking the patent leather of the boot on the floor.

'Well trained you see,' Pamela said.

'But I thought . . .' Karen hesitated. The idea of having a female slave did not excite her at all.

Pamela smiled. 'That's enough. Stand up.'

The maid jumped to her feet.

'That was much better.' Pamela reached forward and ran her hand up under the black skirt of the dress.

'No Mistress, please,' Josephine said at once.

'Don't speak unless you are spoken to,' Pamela snapped. Her hand reached up under the skirt. Karen saw her moving it against the maid's crotch. Josephine began to wriggle uncomfortably, trying to stand still but obviously finding it hard.

'Please, Mistress,' she whispered.

Pamela took her hand away. 'Pull your skirt up.'

The maid reached down to the hem of her skirt and pulled it up to her waist. Karen could not suppress a cry of surprise. She was wearing a black suspender belt clipped onto the tops of fishnet stockings, but she was not wearing panties and hanging down between her legs was a cock. The shaft of the cock was sheathed in a long tube of leather which was laced all the way down its length. The trouble was that this constraint had obviously been applied while the penis was flaccid. The fondling Pamela had given it had made it swell and the cock was now a livid red, the leather biting deeply into the tender flesh. To make matters worse a thin leather thong had been attached to the end of the sheath then tied around the right thigh, forcing the cock downward so it would not spoil the line of the dress.

Karen stared at the spectacle. She felt a strong throb of pleasure from her sex. The man's legs had been shaved and so had his cock and balls, the whole area smooth and hairless.

'Josephine is one of my regulars. He likes to be forced to wear women's clothes. Isn't that right, Josephine?'

'Yes, Miss Pamela.'

'What do you think of my friend, Josephine?'

'She's very beautiful Miss Pamela.'

'She is gorgeous you mean. Now put that thing away and go upstairs to await your punishment.'

The maid pulled the skirt down and scampered out of the room. Karen heard footsteps going upstairs.

'He's really very feminine isn't he?' Pamela said. She got to her feet, collected the bottle of brandy from the cabinet and brought it back to the table, refilling Karen's glass.

'He pays you to do that?'

'Once a week. And every time he comes he begs me not to do it to him. It's fairly easy to work out. Because he's my slave he doesn't have to take responsibility for wanting to cross-dress. He tells himself he only does it because I demand it of him.'

Karen felt like Alice walking through the looking glass. She had stumbled into a whole new world.

'Do you want to see more?'

'More?'

Pamela nodded to the ceiling. 'Upstairs.'

A part of Karen's mind was telling her that she should get out of there, not just walk but run all the way home. But it was out-voted by the strong pulse emanating from her sex; the initial throb of feeling had turned to a persistent ache.

She sipped the brandy. 'What's upstairs?' she asked, her voice coming out as a squeak.

'Another client.'

Karen was surprised at her own reaction. 'I think I'd like that,' she said quite calmly.

Pamela got to her feet and offered Karen her hand. As they touched Karen was aware of an almost electric charge of feeling, her already sensitised body registering another new sensation.

They walked into the hall. The significance of all the pictures was now abundantly clear to Karen. She wondered if any of them featured Pamela's body. Upstairs there was a landing with three doors. Pamela led the way towards the front of the house.

'I just have to change first, won't take a minute,' she said.

She opened the door into what was obviously the master bedroom. It was a large room overlooking the street, which had been beautifully decorated in shades of blue. There was a large bathroom en suite.

Pamela stood in the middle of the room, and without any self-consciousness, pulled down the zip of the silk catsuit that ran down the middle of her back. She pulled her arms out of it then skinned the rest of the garment down her legs. Her big breasts were barely contained in a lacy, black three-quarter cup bra, and she wore matching lace panties with high cut legs, their crotch hardly covering the whole plane of her sex. Her body was a switchback ride for the eye, swelling at her chest, narrowing at her waist, then flaring out again at her voluptuous hips.

Pamela reached behind her back and undid her bra. It fell away from her breasts and they trembled at their freedom. Though they were huge mounds of flesh they did not sag or droop at all but stood out defiantly, like two round globes stuck on to her chest. Oddly, she had rather small nipples and no band of aureole surrounding them.

Hooking her thumbs into the panties Pamela stripped those off too. As she straightened up Karen saw that her red pubic hair had been cut into a neat cigar-like shape on her mons and shaved away completely on her labia. Her belly was round and silky but not slack.

The redhead turned her back on Karen and walked over to the wardrobe that had been built into an alcove of the room, its doors covered in the same blue material that covered the walls. Her buttocks were large ovals of flesh, though they too were not loose and flabby, but solid and firm with what was obviously well-toned muscle. She slid one of the doors open and reached inside, pulling out a black PVC dress. It was short with a corset-type bodice and lacing all the way down both sides.

'This will do,' she said. She stepped into the dress and pulled it on. Her big breasts spilt out of the top while most of her long and meaty thighs were exposed. The lacing at each side also revealed acres of flesh.

Karen had not taken her eyes off Pamela. She felt a swelling of sexual feeling that she didn't want to admit to. It was the same feeling she had had when staring at Barbara's sex on the video. She wondered if it accounted for what she had felt when she had taken Pamela's hand downstairs. It was not something she wanted to think about.

'Come on,' Pamela said.

'What about me?' Karen asked. Her little black dress with a box neck and half sleeves would hardly inspire sexual fervour.

'Oh don't worry about that.'

Pamela led her back on to the landing. She stopped outside the door at the far end. It was painted black and there was a key in the lock. She turned it. 'You sure you want to do this?'

'I'm sure,' Karen said, though this wasn't quite true. The bravado she had displayed downstairs seemed to be seeping away now she had seen Pamela dressed as an out-and-out whore.

Pamela opened the door. The room was completely dark apart from the light spilling in from the hall and Pamela operated a dimmer switch on the wall. A row of spotlights on a rack in the ceiling glowed. Pamela ushered Karen inside and closed the door.

The room was painted black, with black material over the single window and black lino on the floor. Like the room she had seen in the Miltons' video, there was a vertical frame in the centre of the floor. Across the ceiling a wooden beam had been installed and hanging from this was a series of pulleys, chains and white nylon ropes. There was a double bed in one corner behind which was a full-length mirror, and there were two odd wooden contraptions, the purpose of which Karen could only guess. Four metal plates had been bolted to one of the walls and hanging from each of these was a metal ring. It didn't take a lot of imagination to see they were positioned in such a way as to allow Pamela's clients to be spread-eagled against the wall.

'Now you see why I needed a carpenter,' Pamela said.

Standing under the wooden beam was a man. He was naked apart from a pair of what looked like black rubber briefs. His wrists had been tied together behind his back by means of black leather cuffs of the sort Karen had seen Barbara use on Dan. A white nylon rope had been tied into the central link of the cuffs, threaded through one of the pulleys and winched up until his arms were forced into an almost vertical position and he was bent forward, his torso at right angles to his legs. Both of his ankles were strapped into leather cuffs, but these were attached to a three-foot metal rod thus spreading the man's legs wide apart. A thick leather strap around his head held a gag in his mouth and a black silk sleeping mask provided an effective blindfold. Since Pamela had not left her company for one moment over dinner, which had taken well over two hours, it seemed the man had been in this bondage for at least that long.

Kneeling in the left-hand corner of the room, facing the wall, was the maid. He had his hands clasped together behind his back.

'Good evening again, Andrew.'

The captive tried to say something through his gag. It sounded like, 'Good evening,' but the words were muffled.

'I hope you have had time to consider what punishment would be appropriate to your conduct earlier this evening.'

The man nodded his head.

'And what conclusion have you come to?' Pamela

walked up to him. She touched his buttocks and made him start.

He tried to form a word. It sounded like 'six'.

'Six? Did you say six?'

The man nodded violently.

'Well I think that sounds fair. Six with the cane.'

The man shook his head and tried to say no.

'Oh yes Andrew, it has to be the cane.' Pamela looked up at Karen. 'Do you know what he did?'

'No,' Karen said. She saw the man react immediately to the sound of her voice, moving his head as if trying to work out where she was standing in the room.

'Oh, I forgot to tell you Andrew. We have a visitor. A beautiful new friend of mine. Karen, this is Andrew.'

'Good evening Andrew,' Karen said in a slightly mocking tone, surprised at how calm she sounded.

'What do you say, Andrew?'

'Good evening, Mistress,' he said, though each word was again muffled.

'Andrew dared to touch me without permission. Can you imagine that? He touched my leg. That's true isn't it Andrew?'

The man nodded almost imperceptibly.

'And now he has to be punished for his impertinence.'

Pamela walked up to Karen, smiled then went to a large wooden cupboard behind the door. She opened it and took out a long, thin rattan cane with a curved handle, just like the type that had long been banned from use in schools.

'Shall we give him a treat?' she asked Karen. 'Shall we let him see you?'

'I don't mind,' Karen said. It was true. All her trepidation had disappeared. She felt excited and alive.

'Do you want to see my friend, Andrew?'

He nodded.

Pamela pulled the silk mask off his face. He blinked once or twice to get used to the light but it was dim and he soon recovered the use of his sight. He turned his head and stared at Karen.

'Now it's punishment time.'

Pamela took hold of the waistband of the pants and wrestled them down until the black rubber banded his thighs. Without a word, Pamela raised the cane. Bound as he was there was absolutely nothing he could do to protect himself. She slashed it down on the man's upturned buttocks. They were quite fleshy and quivered as the cane cut across them, leaving a bright pink stripe. The man cried out loud.

Karen felt her clit pulse sharply. As little as a week ago she would have been totally shocked by everything she had seen. Now it had an altogether different effect on her.

Thwack. Thwack. Two more strokes landed in quick succession. The whole of the man's buttocks turned pink, but there were three distinct thin stripes in an even deeper red.

'Do you want to try?' Pamela asked, holding out the cane.

Karen hesitated then took it from her hand. 'I'll try,' she said.

She positioned herself behind the bound man. She remembered how the thought of Dan's helplessness on the video had excited her, and this time she was faced with the real thing. Haltingly, as if to reassure herself that he was real, she put out her hand and touched his back.

'Feel his bum,' Pamela said, 'feel the heat.'

Karen lowered her hand to the man's bottom. It was

radiating heat like a fire. She felt another sharp pang from her clitoris.

'Go on,' Pamela encouraged.

Karen raised the cane and brought it down fiercely on the man's rear. He cried out through the gag, his whole bottom quivering. But his reaction was no less intense than her own. An electric shock of sensation seemed to travel up the cane to her arm then branch out to her most sensitive nerves. Her nipples puckered and she felt her sex contract strongly. Without waiting to be prompted this time she raised the cane again. Thwack. The man's buttocks quivered and he cried out and Karen felt another intense wave of feeling course through her body.

'One more,' Pamela said.

Karen suddenly felt weak. Her sex had become sticky and wet and she had an almost irresistible urge to pull up her skirt and finger her clit. She tried to pull herself together and raised the cane, cutting it down right across the meat of his buttocks with perhaps the hardest stroke of all. The man wailed through the gag.

When Karen looked up at Pamela she saw the redhead looking at her critically, as if trying to judge what her reaction might be. A flicker of a knowing smile broke her lips.

'Well?' Pamela whispered in her ear. She put her hand on Karen's arm and caused another electric shock of feeling, just as her touch had downstairs.

'I've never felt like this before,' Karen whispered back.

Pamela smiled. 'So it seems the experiment is a success. Do you want to go now while I finish him off?'

'I want to stay,' Karen said. Leaving now was the last thing that was on her mind.

'All right. Aren't you the lucky one Andrew? My friend is going to stay and watch.'

Pamela went to the cleat where the rope from the pulley was tied off and unwound it, allowing the rope to fall. The man's bound wrists were lowered until he was able to stand up straight again. The front of the rubber pants had hooked themselves around his large erection and still covered it completely.

'Josephine,' Pamela barked. 'Undo the rope from the pulley and his ankles.'

The maid sprang to his feet. He came around behind Andrew and quickly unfastened the white nylon rope from the cuffs then unstrapped his ankles.

'On the floor.'

Andrew, who was clearly having trouble co-ordinating his limbs after so long in such tight bondage, managed to get to the floor and lay on his back. Naturally, with his arms still bound behind him his body was bowed awkwardly, with his belly higher than his shoulders and legs. The contact of his reddened bottom with the floor made him squirm his hips from side to side. Pamela strode over to him, wriggled up the tight skirt of the dress an inch or two to allow her to comfortably spread her legs apart then placed her feet on either side of his shoulders. As she was wearing no panties Andrew would be staring right up into her sex.

She winked at Karen. 'I have to get a little pleasure too,' she said. Slowly, she squatted down until her sex was an inch or more from Andrew's mouth. For the second time in so many days Karen watched a helplessly bound man licking at the sex of a totally dominant woman. But this was not a picture on a television screen; it was real. She saw the man's tongue wriggling against Pamela's clit and heard the redhead's little gasps of pleasure.

'Faster,' she said testily.

Andrew tried to obey, moving his head from side to side as well as flicking his tongue. Pamela moaned then pressed herself down on his mouth until his whole face disappeared in the large expanse of her buttocks. Then she rolled her hips, grinding herself down on him.

After a minute of this she relented and lifted herself slightly. Andrew's face was red and he was panting. But as he desperately gulped air down Pamela descended again. She held herself there much longer this time and Andrew's body began to buck and twist, trying somehow to find a way to breathe.

When she lifted herself for the second time his face was as red as his bottom had been. He gasped in air. This time she leant forward slightly and pulled at the front of the rubber pants, freeing the top half of his erection but leaving the bottom half still covered in rubber, holding it down against his belly. Then she leant back and settled her sex down on his mouth and nose again.

'You have my permission,' she said.

Karen saw his body tense as it used up the little oxygen he'd been able to suck in. At the same time Pamela was grinding her sex down on his face, moving her clitoris across the thick bone of his chin. She moaned loudly and screwed her eyes closed. The whole of her body seemed to quiver.

At that exact moment Andrew's cock spasmed violently against the tightness of the rubber that cut across it. A jet of white spunk arced out of it and up over his belly.

Pamela opened her eyes, steadied herself with her

hand on his chest and got to her feet as Andrew sucked in much needed air.

'Quite a performance don't you think?' she said, grinning broadly.

Chapter Three

FINALLY SATED KAREN lay in bed feeling completely exhausted. It was not surprising. She had just had three orgasms in the space of five minutes. With the Miltons asleep in the next door bedroom she had had to stuff a pair of her panties into her mouth to suppress the screams of ecstasy that she's made as she'd thrust the handle of her hairbrush – the only implement that she could find that vaguely resembled a phallus – into her vagina with one hand, while she frotted her clitoris with the other.

Her mind was full of images. She could see Andrew's body bent double by the tight bondage and his buttocks vibrating under the strokes of the cane. She could see his cock, half-tangled up in the black rubber panties, ejaculating over his belly, and the cross-dressing maid standing with his black skirt held up around his waist and his cock straining against the tight leather restraint.

But there were other images too which were more disturbing. In the deepest throes of orgasm she had pictured Pamela standing in her bedroom stripping off her clothes, her big breasts trembling, and imagined her lowering her sex on to Andrew's mouth.

Despite her tiredness Karen could not sleep and lay in bed allowing the little tremors of the aftermath of orgasm to play through her body. She was finding it hard to accept what she had seen tonight. She supposed it was fair to say that Pamela was a prostitute, selling sexual services for money. But prostitution to her had always seemed sordid and dirty. The way Pamela had behaved was certainly sexually uncompromising but Karen could see absolutely nothing wrong with it. The men quite clearly got exactly what they paid for and Pamela was not cynical about what she did.

But the experiment, as Pamela had called it, had left little doubt in Karen's mind, that she shared Pamela's – and Barbara's – proclivities. The idea that she could have a man completely at her mercy as Andrew had been last night excited her in a way nothing else ever had. She spent the small hours of the morning, until the dawn came leaking through the bedroom curtains and the birds began to sing, trying to work out why but couldn't come up with a single reason. She had never been aware of the slightest inclination in that direction before and could think of nothing in her short life that would have made her want to be sexually dominant over men. But she had to face the fact that that was what she wanted.

If she was being absolutely honest with herself, there was something else she had to face up to as well. While she had watched the video of the Miltons and been with Pamela, she had undoubtedly felt another distinct sexual emotion. She had been strongly attracted to both women. Seeing their naked bodies she had felt an intense desire to touch them, fondle and caress them and be touched, fondled and caressed in return. She had never felt anything like that before, but as much as she wished she could deny it, put it down to the fact that she was experiencing the most powerful sexual emotions she had ever had, she knew that a distinct part of it had been the very definite craving to press her lips against Pamela's mouth and crush her own body into hers.

How she dealt with that – or her desire to be dominant – she didn't know. In one sense she hoped they would both go away. Her life hadn't been so bad without these mind-blowing orgasms. But the truth was that lethargy was not an option. In her heart of hearts she knew she had opened up a box of delights for herself that she just had to explore. The only question was when and how.

'Roger, how nice,' Karen said, slipping into the tan leather seat of Roger's open-topped Jaguar.

'Hi,' he said, kissing her on the cheek.

Roger Howard had called her at work that afternoon and asked her if she was free for dinner. She was glad of the distraction. She had been brooding over recent events for two days now and going out with him would give her a break from her own thoughts. She'd asked him to pick her up from home at seven o'clock. He'd been right on time.

'Where do you want to go?' he asked.

'How about your flat?' she said.

He looked at her sideways on. They had been out three times before but she had never shown the slightest inclination to want to come home with him. 'I thought you wanted to eat?' he said.

'I do. But I'd like to see where you live. If you'd rather not . . .'

'No, I'd like that. It's not far.'

'Good.'

Roger put the Jaguar into gear and drove off toward Hammersmith. Turning left he headed towards Kensington where he had a flat in one of the older and grander mansion blocks.

'So what have you been up to?' she asked, enjoying the feeling of the air blowing in her long blonde hair.

'Nothing much. And you?'

Roger was a merchant banker, with a family pedigree to match; his father was an earl or a duke and his mother's family had an estate in Northumberland the size of the Isle of Wight. They had met at the agency where he was trying to find a regular cleaner for his flat. When she heard he worked in the City she'd asked if he'd mind her picking his brains about job prospects and they'd ended up having dinner together.

'Oh, I've been having a really exciting time,' she said teasingly. She pressed her tongue against her upper lip.

'Sounds great, what have you been up to?'

'I think it's what you call a voyage of discovery,' she said. 'I've been finding out things about myself that I never knew.'

'Like what?'

'Wouldn't you like to know,' she said. Exactly how much, if anything, she was going to reveal to him tonight she had no idea. But she was in the mood to experiment again and Roger Howard had provided the ideal opportunity.

They parked outside the mansion block and rode up in a rackety old iron-caged lift.

His apartment was large and spacious and all his furniture was ancient or antique, no doubt family heirlooms donated from their various homes. There was an old sofa in the sitting room, an even older armchair with big patches on the arms, and an oak sideboard.

Only the television and video recorder looked as if they were brand new.

'I've never been that interested in décor. I suppose I should get someone in to fix the place up,' he explained, seeing the sitting room through her eyes.

'How about the bedroom? You have got a bed, I take it?'

'Yes,' he said in a puzzled tone.

'Show me then,' she said. 'Or are you too shy?' Considering they had only managed a rather modest kiss on their last date she could understand the look of surprise on his face. The trouble was he exuded a hint of terror too. 'Don't be frightened, I won't bite,' she said. 'Not unless it's called for.'

She had never behaved like this with a man but was enjoying every minute of it. In the past she had always allowed men to make all the running, waiting for them to set the sexual pace. What she had seen Pamela and Barbara do had somehow given her the confidence to assert her own agenda.

He led her down the hall to his bedroom. It was a large rectangular room with a spectacular view over Holland Park. He had a modern-looking double bed, though the built-in bedside tables and matching wardrobes that surrounded it looked as though they had been built in the Fifties. There was an en suite bathroom covered in large white tiles, with an enamelled bath and a huge wash basin. The toilet was so old-fashioned it had an overhead cistern and a chain.

'Why don't you go into the bathroom for a few minutes,' she said. 'There's no telling what you might find when you come out.' She kissed him delicately on the cheek then changed her mind and caught his face in both her hands, pressing his mouth into hers.

'Do you really want to do this?' he said.

'Is that so strange?'

'No, it's just that . . .' His voice tailed off. Dutifully he walked to the bathroom. She could not get over the impression that he did it with an air of reluctance.

Karen pulled the heavy velvet curtains over the window and turned on the bedside light. She was wearing a button-through grey cotton dress which she quickly discarded. As a trainee in the firm her salary left her very little money to spare but she had had enough to buy a pair of glossy black hold-up stockings from a shop in Notting Hill. She had also found a pair of thong-cut black satin panties and was wearing her highest heeled shoes. She had dressed for sex. What sort of sex was another matter.

She took off her bra, which didn't match her panties, and lay in the middle of the bed, her own bravado making her feel almost breathless. Taking off her panties, she decided, was a step too far.

Roger knocked at the bathroom door. 'Are you ready?' he asked timorously.

'Ah ha . . .' she said.

The door opened and Roger emerged wearing a white towel knotted around his waist. He was a fairly short man, and though he was not fat she could see he had the beginnings of a paunch developing around his stomach. His chest was hairless though his arms and legs were covered with a light mat of hair. His face was not unattractive, with a small nose and chin but quite big brown eyes, and his straight brown hair was parted at the side.

'You look stunning,' he said, gazing at her body. She could see his eyes moving over her breasts and down her legs to the black tops of the stockings. She scissored her legs apart allowing him to examine the black satin that was stretched tightly over her sex.

'Thank you,' she said. She patted the bed at her side. 'Come over here Roger.' She tried out a much more authoritative tone. Apparently it worked. He trotted over to the bed and sat down. 'Now kiss me.'

He leant forward and kissed her gently on the lips. But she was not in the mood for gentleness and she wrapped a hand around his neck and crushed their lips together. When she felt his tongue enter her mouth she sucked on it hard, while her hand moved over his naked back.

He rolled on to the bed beside her and she felt the hardness of his cock growing rapidly against her hip. Her hand loosened the towel then moved down over his buttocks.

'Lovely tits,' he said, breaking the kiss and moving his mouth down over her collarbone. He sucked in her nipple and the surrounding breast, then began flicking at the little hard button of flesh with his tongue, producing ripples of pleasure in Karen's body.

'Wonderful,' she said.

He moved to the other breast and did the same thing, then trailed his tongue down over her belly, licking and sucking and nibbling at her flesh. She could feel her clitoris throbbing as he got closer to the waistband of her panties. He slid his hands over her waist and began rolling the panties down over her hips. She lifted her buttocks to allow him to pull them off, then raised her left foot and extracted it from the flimsy garment. He left the panties there, wrapped around her right knee, as he buried his face between her legs. She felt a huge pulse of pleasure as his tongue wriggled between her labia and butted against her clit.

'Mmm . . .'

He was good at this. The tip of his tongue circled her clit a few times then began to flick it from side to side.

At the same time she felt his fingers working up under her thighs until they were positioned at the mouth of her wet vagina. She felt one then two pushing inside, thrusting up until his knuckles were hard against her labia. He began fucking her with them, pulling them in and out at exactly the same pace as he was using to batter her clit with his tongue. His other hand slid back up toward her breasts, his fingers squeezing the mounds of flesh one after the other before he pinched at her nipples again, dividing his attention equally between both of them.

The three distinct feelings begin to coalesce. It was wonderful. Somewhere just behind her clit a hard knot of pleasure was throbbing continuously, fed by the sensations Roger was generating in her vagina, her nipples and in her clit itself. But the odd thing was she knew she was nowhere near to having an orgasm. The feelings were better than anything she'd experienced before with a man, but had none of the shattering power of the orgasms she'd given herself over the last few days.

She closed her eyes. There, waiting in the darkness for her, was Andrew's bound body and his red, cane-striped arse. And there was Pamela in the tight PVC mini-dress, her big breasts spilling over the bodice, squatting above him as his tongue did exactly what Roger's tongue was doing to her now. The feelings in Karen's body immediately shifted into a higher gear.

She knew what she needed now. She opened her eyes again.

'Fuck me now, Roger,' she said. 'I need it.'

He looked disappointed, as if he had hoped he could bring her off like this, but obediently he raised his head, slid his fingers out of her sex and started to roll on top of her.

58

That was very definitely not what she wanted.

'No,' she said, pushing him back, 'I like to be on top.' She had never said that to any man before, and had never actually done it either. But remembering how Barbara had straddled Dan's hips she sat up and swung one leg over Roger's body, posing her sex above his cock. She took it in her hand. It was not as large or as distressed as either Dan's or Andrew's had been and she wondered how he would react if she suggested she strapped it into a leather harness.

She shook her shoulders from side to side, making her breasts slap into each other. This produced a huge wave of feeling in her nipples that travelled down to her clit and made that spasm too. Looking down at him she tried to imagine that he was spread-eagled across the bed, his wrists and ankles strapped into leather cuffs, his mouth gagged with her panties.

Trying to push aside all the images that were assailing her she guided his cock between her labia and slowly eased herself down on to it.

'That's so good,' she said, pressing her fingers into her belly. 'I can feel it right here.'

She pulled herself up until his glans almost slipped out of her then dropped down on him with all her weight, enjoying the feeling of him pushing the silky wet walls of her vagina apart. She pushed her belly forward so his cock was dragged towards the front of her sex then pulled herself up again. Thrusting down on him she pulled herself back too, starting a sort of circular motion: forward and up, backward and down, forcing his cock into every part of her sex.

But though she was on top and had a real cock inside her, hot and throbbing, the feelings her body was generating were nothing like the intensity of those that the handle of her hairbrush had provoked. She tried harder, increasing the rhythm of her movement, pushing down, grasping her own breasts and pinching viciously at her nipples with her fingernails, but it was not enough.

'Give me your hands,' she said. She grabbed them before he could comply and leant forward, stretching them up above his head and spreading them apart, while thrusting back on his cock at the same time. But it did not create the illusion she yearned for. He was not helpless; he was not bound.

He must have sensed that she was disappointed. 'Let me,' he said.

And she did. Wrapping her arms around him he rolled her over on to her back with his cock still inside her and began pumping into her. It was what all her lovers had done to her before and it produced the same response. She felt mild tingles of pleasure in her sex and in her clit but they were muted and would certainly not lead to an orgasm.

Karen closed her eyes. Quite deliberately this time she pictured herself walking into Pamela's treatment room. She saw the maid kneeling in the corner and the bound body of Andrew standing so awkwardly in the middle of the room. She watched as Pamela administered the cane then turned and handed it to her, remembered the look on Pamela's face. It was challenging, daring her to cross a threshold. She could almost feel her fingers wrapping around the thin bamboo.

'Oh God.' Suddenly her sex was alive. She pushed down on Roger's cock as he thrust forward.

'Yes, yes,' he said, taking her new enthusiasm as a token of his success.

Now she was raising the cane, aiming it. She saw it hit, and watched Andrew's buttocks convulse, his limbs straining to escape against his bondage but with no possibility of doing so.

Roger was coming. She could feel his cock pulsing violently inside her and then she was coming too. Her hands circled his buttocks, her fingers digging into his flesh as if to urge him deeper. Her vagina clenched around him, and as she felt thick gobs of spunk spattering into the depths of her, a sharp, almost painful orgasm shot through every nerve, making her whole body shudder. And there, swirling in the middle of all the tremors of pleasure, she saw Pamela, standing naked, her big breasts held proud. Despite the weight on top of her she arched herself up off the bed, thrusting her sex against his cock to wring every last ounce from the extraordinary feelings that were pulsing through her.

'Christ, that was something,' Roger said, rolling off her. 'My God, Karen, I had no idea.'

'No idea about what?'

'That you were so sexy.'

'Well now you know.' She found she could not look him straight in the eye. He had been the instrument of her pleasure but not the progenitor. She had used him in much the same way she had used the handle of her hairbrush.

'Shall we go and get something to eat? I'm starving.' He leapt out of bed looking incredibly pleased with himself.

She supposed other women would have found him a more than adequate lover, and a week ago she would have been of the same opinion. She would have laid there passively on her back and have experienced nothing more than a mild sensation of pleasure. But as she got up and reached for her bra she realised that things had changed irrevocably now. She had found a means through which to give herself the sort of sexual gratification that she had only read about before. Exactly how far she was prepared to go in the pursuit of that gratification was a different matter entirely.

'Hi, how are you?'

Karen recognised Pamela's voice. She was pleased to hear from her. It had been five days since she had gone to dinner at her house.

'I'm fine. And you?'

'Oh, I'm really enjoying living in this part of London. It's great. Listen, I'll tell you why I'm calling. Can anyone overhear this?'

'No.' Pamela was calling on Karen's private line.

'Good. I just wondered how you felt about our little experiment.'

'To tell you the truth Pamela I felt great about it.'

'No ill effects or afterthoughts?'

'None.'

'Great. In that case I thought that this might interest you. I've got a client who likes to be watched, if you know what I mean.'

'I think I can imagine.'

'Well, I thought if you'd like to earn a little extra money you might fit the bill. He'd pay two hundred pounds.'

'Two hundred pounds!' Karen cried in surprise. She looked around in case anyone had heard her. Fortunately everyone was too busy.

'Yes. Is that enough?'

'Enough? It's too much.'

'Don't be silly. Are you interested?'

Karen did not hesitate. 'Of course.'

'Tomorrow night, at seven.'

'I'll be there.'

'Well that's settled. It'll be nice to see you again. Are you sure?'

'Positive.' And Karen found that was absolutely true.

'See you tomorrow then.'

As she put the phone down Karen was aware of a strong pulse of feeling emanating from her sex. The thought of seeing Pamela again, let alone one of her submissive clients, was incredibly exciting.

Karen tried not to think too much about it and get on with her work. It was nearly five o'clock in the afternoon and she had several things to do before going home at six. On the bus later, however, it was difficult not to start speculating about what Pamela had said, as well as wondering how she would spend the money. It had been a long time since she'd had two hundred pounds to spend without having to divide it up to meet her expenses. Perhaps she could buy some new lingerie!

She wondered exactly what would be required of her. The only clue Pamela had given was that the man liked to be 'watched'. Presumably, as a dedicated slave, he wanted her to watch as Pamela put him through his paces. That was certainly an interesting prospect.

'So how are you getting on at Angels sweetie? We haven't really had a chance to talk in the last couple of weeks.'

Karen had arrived home to find that Dan was away at some business conference in the Midlands and that Barbara was all alone. They had eaten dinner and shared a bottle of white wine and were now sitting on the sofa in the sitting room, with a second bottle open in front of them. The weather had changed for the better and they had the back windows open, a slight and balmy breeze bringing the scent of summer flowers into the room.

'I love it there. Malcolm is very complimentary about my work and all the staff are really nice.'

'Do you think you'll stay there then?'

'God no. I'm enjoying myself at the moment but I wouldn't want to do it for the rest of my life. I've been writing off for jobs in the City. I've written fifty letters and only had three replies. I'll just have to keep trying. I thought perhaps I might go to university and try and get a business administration degree. But I'd prefer just to get stuck in.'

'Why are you so keen on the City?'

'I don't know. It's always been an ambition of mine and I think you should always try and go for what you want, don't you?'

There was a pause. Karen had the feeling Barbara wanted to say something but was hesitating.

'More wine?'

'I shouldn't really but I will.' Karen held out her glass and Barbara refilled it.

'Look Karen,' she said eventually. 'About that tape.'

Karen smiled. 'What about it?' She had noticed that all the numbered tapes had disappeared from the cabinet in the sitting room.

'I just hope you don't think badly of me, that's all. I mean you've had more time to think about it now.'

'Of course, and I don't. Quite the reverse. It was amazing.'

'Really?'

'Yes. I don't think I'd really thought much about sex before. I mean about the sort of things people do.' She had no intention of telling her about Pamela, not yet at least. 'It was an eye opener. And I'd like to see more.'

'What!'

'I'd love to see another tape. It's a good job you hid them away or I'd have put one on the other night when you went out to dinner.'

'Really?'

'Dan's a very attractive man and you are a superb specimen of a woman. It's not surprising, is it? Seeing the two of you together like that was a real turn on for me. I'd love to see more.'

'Are you serious?'

'Of course.'

Barbara sipped her wine. Karen could see that she was thinking, trying to work out implications and consequences. 'Hold on a minute then.' She got to her feet and left the room. A few minutes later she came back carrying a video cassette. 'As we're alone, if you really want to . . .'

'I do.'

Barbara knelt in front of the video and slotted the cassette into it. She came back to the sofa with the remote control in her hand, then pressed the play button.

The screen flicked into life.

'Have you shown these to anyone else?' Karen asked.

'There's a little circle of us with similar interests. We swap videos.'

Karen saw the grey room appear on the television screen. The camera was focused on Dan, who stood against the bare wall. Once again he was naked but this time his chest was adorned with a heavy metal chain attached to two clips that had been fastened to his nipples. Instead of the complicated harness around his cock, this time there was a single strap that was wound around the bottom of his shaft and under his balls. His wrists were held together by metal handcuffs and drawn over his head where the handcuffs had been fastened to a metal ring set in the wall. His ankles were spread apart and strapped into the leather cuffs Karen had seen before, each fastened by a small chain to rings set into the wall just above the skirting board.

'I think we should make good use of that mouth of yours, don't you?'

It was Barbara's voice but as yet she could not be seen.

'Yes, Mistress Barbara.'

Barbara walked into the shot. She was wearing a pair of cream-coloured stockings with a fully fashioned heel and a seam picked out in black, and a wide lacy suspender belt stretched tautly over her thighs. She wore nothing else but a pair of spiky stiletto shoes in white leather, her firm, round buttery breasts completely naked.

Standing at Dan's side so the camera would be able to see exactly what she was doing she picked up the metal chain and pulled it towards Dan's mouth. He groaned. Karen could see the clips stretching his nipples, the metal cutting deeply into his already tortured flesh.

'Hold it in your mouth,' she said.

'No, Mistress, please,' he begged, but from the way his cock was twitching Karen could see he obviously derived a great deal of pleasure from the pain.

'Do as I say,' Barbara snapped.

Dan held the chain between his lips.

'Drop it and you're in trouble,' Barbara said. She grasped his cock in her right hand and squeezed it, making the glans balloon out from the top of her fist. 'Does it hurt?' she asked.

He nodded his head, slightly afraid that if he did it too violently he would lose hold of the chain.

'So sensitive,' she mocked, letting go of his cock and dropping to her knees. She extended her tongue and stroked it against the tip of his glans, licking off the little drop of fluid that had formed there. 'Do you want me to suck it right in?' she asked.

Again he nodded carefully.

Immediately she sunk her mouth right down on his shaft, until her lips were grazing his pubic hair. She sucked on it so hard Karen could see her cheeks dimple. Dan moaned. Barbara drew back, then ran her tongue around the distinct ridge at the base of his glans.

'You want it so badly don't you?'

'Yes, Mistress Barbara,' he tried to say without losing his grip on the chain.

'Too bad, because you're not going to get it. I've got a little surprise for you.'

She got to her feet and strode off across the room and out of the picture.

'Are you sure you want to go on?' Barbara asked.

Karen was so engrossed in the film that it was a shock to hear Barbara's voice coming from her side. She looked at her friend. 'Of course.'

On screen there was the sound of a door being opened and Karen saw Dan's face staring intently off camera. It was soon obvious what he was staring at. A woman entered the picture. She was, Karen thought, about the same age as Barbara and had the same long, jet-black hair that was parted in the middle and fell to her shoulders. She was wearing a black, almost transparent, lace basque with a three-quarter cup bra and black satin suspenders. Her slender legs were sheathed in very sheer black stockings and she wore the seemingly obligatory ultra high-heeled shoes, these in classy black suede. Like Barbara she was not wearing panties and her mons was covered with a patch of thick black hair so perfectly triangular it looked as though it had been carefully trimmed.

'So this is Dan, is it?' she said, striding across the room. 'Nice nipple clips. Do they hurt?' She took the chain from his lips and pulled it higher. Dan groaned. 'I'm Mistress Jessica,' she said. 'I've come to see how well behaved you can be.'

She dropped the chain and took hold of Dan's cock. 'A nice weapon,' she said.

Barbara entered the shot on the other side of her husband. 'Don't you think she's beautiful?'

The surprise and shock on Dan's face was so marked that Karen was sure this had not been rehearsed ahead of time.

'Yes,' he said.

'Yes, what?' Jessica snapped, slapping his cock with the palm of her hand. 'Don't tell me you're not properly trained.'

'Yes, Mistress Barbara,' he intoned at once.

'That's better,' Jessica said. She took hold of the clips at either end of the chain. 'I'm going to take these off now. At the count of three. One, two, three.' She pinched the clips and pulled them away. The pain of taking them off must have been worse than having them on and Dan gasped, his body trembling. 'Let's get him down from there and have some fun.'

'Actually,' Barbara said with a real sparkle in her eye, 'there was something else I thought we could do.'

'Oh really, and what might that be?'

To Karen's amazement, Barbara took Jessica's hand and drew her into her arms. Despite the heels she was a good two or three inches shorter so Barbara had to lower her head slightly as she brought her lips to the girl's rather thin mouth and kissed her passionately, squirming their mouths together less than a foot away from her husband.

Karen felt herself blushing. She dare not glance to her right to see what the real Barbara was doing for fear that she was watching her reaction. She swallowed hard and stared at the screen.

The two women pressed their bodies together, their arms wrapping around their backs, Barbara's leg moving up between Jessica's so her thigh was ironed against her naked sex. Barbara's breasts were crushed flat by Jessica's more modest chest under the lace basque. Karen could see Dan watching them both intently, a look of total astonishment on his face.

'This was the first time,' the real Barbara said by way of explanation. 'Over a year ago now.'

On screen the two women broke apart.

'Mmm . . . that was nice,' Jessica said. 'I always suspected you wanted to do that.' She raised her hand and touched Barbara's breasts one after the other gently tweaking her nipples. 'Wish I had tits like that.'

'They're all yours,' Barbara said, laughing. 'Come on, I've got an idea.'

The screen went fuzzy. A moment later it cleared again. The wooden frame that Karen had seen in the first video had been pulled over to the centre of the room, so it was right in front of Dan's bound body, and a thin mattress covered the wooden slats. Still in the lacy basque, stockings and high heels, Jessica was laying on the bed with her black hair spread out across the mattress and her feet less than a metre away from Dan's body. Barbara came into the shot. She knelt on the bed and, with her back to the camera, straddled Jessica's shoulders. She allowed the other woman to stare up at her sex for a moment, then lowered herself until her hairless labia were touching her lips, almost as if they were kissing them.

Karen saw Jessica move her hands around Barbara's thigh and lever herself up, pressing her mouth against Barbara's pubic bone and appearing to gnaw on it quite aggressively. Barbara moaned loudly, pressing her hands into her breasts, flattening them against her rib cage. Then Jessica pulled back slightly and started tapping her tongue against Barbara's swollen clit.

The effect on Karen's sex was almost as dramatic as she was sure it had been on Barbara's. Her clitoris pulsed wildly and she felt a sharp pang of excitement deep inside her vagina. As much as she had tried not to think about the desire she had felt for both Barbara and Pamela it was impossible to ignore when it was thrust so explicitly in front of her.

On screen Karen could see the expression on Dan's face. The shock and surprise had gone. Now the only discernible emotion was lust, his eyes rooted on the two women. His cock was a vivid red, and was standing up almost vertically.

Karen suddenly realised that Jessica had a large, black rubber dildo in her hand. She recognised it immediately; it was the largest of those she had seen in Barbara's bedside drawer. Jessica brought it up behind Barbara and pushed it between the cheeks of her arse. Barbara leant forward, supporting herself on her arms with her hands either side of Jessica's knees. This position enabled the camera to see Jessica inserting the tip of the dildo into the slit of Barbara's labia. She thrust it forward until the whole phallus has disappeared and only the butt end could be seen, with Barbara's inner labia pouted around it, then returned her tongue to Barbara's clit. Barbara moaned loudly then dropped her head down between Jessica's thighs and applied her mouth to the girl's sex. At the same time she snaked her hand under the girl's thigh and pressed her fingers up into her vagina.

Dan looked on helplessly. He tried to pull his hand-cuffs away from the ring in the wall, chaffing the metal against his wrists. He was bucking his hips rhythmi-cally, his cock trying desperately to fuck thin air.

The two women were so wrapped up in themselves they hardly noticed him. Their bodies seemed to melt together, wriggling sinuously against each other, prone to the same sensations. Karen could see their eager mouths licking and sucking at each other's clits as Jessica plied the big dildo in and out of Barbara's vagina. They were both making noises too, moans, groans, little yelps of pleasure, a growing crescendo of sound. It was obvious they were coming, the move-ments of their bodies getting more pronounced as the volume of sound increased.

Suddenly Barbara's body went rigid. She raised her head, opened her mouth and made a throaty rattling noise as Karen saw Jessica thrust the dildo into her one more time. She held it there with the flat of her hand as her tongue relentlessly circled Barbara's clit.

'Yes, yes . . .' Barbara screamed, looking directly at her husband.

Jessica was not far behind. As soon as the crisis of her orgasm had passed Barbara lowered her head again and went back to work on Jessica's sex. In seconds Karen saw Jessica's head arc backward on the mattress and she cried out loud, her body trembling violently.

They did not stop, however. The first orgasm only seemed to give them an appetite for a second. Abandoning the dildo this time, Jessica thrust her fingers into Barbara's body. Two went into her vagina and a third into the perfectly circular and puckered ring of her arse. Their bodies swayed and undulated against each other, Barbara's breasts squashed so flat they were squeezed out at the side of her body. This time they appeared to come together, the moans of ecstasy muffled against each other's intimate flesh.

Barbara rolled off Jessica. They both sat up, looking at Dan.

'He's in a terrible state,' Jessica said.

It was true. Dan's cock looked red raw and fluid was dripping from the end of it. He was sweating too, beads of perspiration running from his forehead down on to his chest.

Jessica got to her knees in front of him and licked the sticky fluid from his glans with her tongue.

'I think it's his turn now don't you?' she said, grinning.

Barbara got to her feet and reached up above Dan's head, freeing the handcuffs from the metal ring, though leaving his wrists still bound together. She released the ankle cuffs too.

Jessica knelt on all fours on the bed, her knees spread apart, manoeuvring herself, Karen suspected quite deliberately, so that she was exactly sideways on to the camera.

Barbara wiped the sweat from her husband's forehead, then pushed him down on the bed, so he was kneeling behind Jessica.

'She's beautiful, isn't she?'

'Yes, Mistress Barbara.' His voice was oddly flat and emotionless as if his ability to form words was failing him.

Karen could imagine the view Dan was presented with: Jessica's open sex framed by the black lingerie and stockings.

'Fuck her then,' Barbara said. 'Make her come.'

Dan looked at her as if he could not believe what he was hearing but he did not need any further encouragement. He put his handcuffed hands on the top of

Jessica's back and prodded his cock between her legs. Jessica moaned loudly.

'He's so hot.'

'All that waiting's made him bigger too. Really swollen.'

Dan bucked his hips and Karen saw the long reddened shaft of his cock disappear into Jessica's body. He began to plough it into her as she thrust her buttocks back at him.

For a moment Barbara stepped out of the picture. She returned with a riding crop in her hand. She raised the crop and slashed it down on Dan's buttocks, making him thrust forward much more urgently.

'Yes,' Jessica said, raising her head until it was almost at right angles to her spine.

Barbara struck again. Dan cried out this time as his cock was skewered into Jessica's sex by the impact of the blow.

'Oh god . . .' Jessica screamed. She thrust back on the rock hard and red-hot phallus that was buried so deep inside her and came. Karen saw her head drop and her body go rigid, every muscle taut.

Barbara pulled her husband back until he was completely clear of Jessica's sex then callously grabbed his phallus. She ringed it with her fingers and wanked it up and down no more than once or twice before it spasmed violently and an arc of white spunk shot out, spattering down on Jessica's buttocks and the back of the lacy basque. A second, less violent spending seemed to hit the lips of her sex, producing a huge shudder of sensation in her body. Barbara squeezed his cock, milking every last drop out of him, spunk oozing over her fingers.

'Aren't you a lucky boy,' she said, looking straight into the camera.

The picture went fuzzy. The real Barbara reached forward and pressed the remote control. The whirling of the video recorder stopped. She refilled both their glasses without saying a word, then picked up her own.

'I selected that one especially,' she said quietly. 'I thought you should know the whole truth about me.'

'That you're bisexual you mean?' Karen said.

'Yes. Are you shocked?'

'No.' Karen selected her words carefully. She would have liked to tell Barbara about her own feelings, the effect that seeing both her and Pamela naked had had on her. But she still wasn't sure whether she was ready to admit to those feelings yet. So she said, 'I don't think it matters what you do. And Dan clearly enjoyed himself. Has this been going on long?'

'No, not really. Like I told you, we found a little group of people who like to indulge in the same sort of sexual . . .' She tried to think of the right word, '. . . activities. Jessica organises it. Most of the women seemed to be bisexual. I thought I'd give it a try and I found I got very turned on by it especially if Dan was watching. Jessica's beautiful, don't you think?'

'Very.'

'Anyway, now you know. Don't worry, I'm not going to jump on you. I'm not a lesbian. I'd never even imagined doing it with a woman, not once.'

'I think I can appreciate that,' Karen said, understanding only too well.

'I've only ever done it with Dan watching. That makes it different; at least I like to kid myself that it does.'

'Don't you get jealous, seeing him with another woman?'

'That would be hypocritical wouldn't it, after he's

74

watched me with one? What's sauce for the goose . . . I get what I want, so there's no harm in him sharing some of it, as long as I'm in control. And . . .' She hesitated.

'Yes?' Karen prompted.

'Jessica organises parties too sometimes. It's not just videos we swap. I like to see him being put through his paces.' There was a real sparkle in Barbara's eye. 'Now you're really shocked.'

'No I'm not. I believe people should be free to do whatever they like sexually. It's just not something I've come across before. Look, I think I'd better be getting to bed. I've got a lot to do tomorrow and I'm going out in the evening,' Karen said.

'I'm going up too.' Barbara got to her feet. There was, not surprisingly, a certain awkwardness in the air.

'How long's Dan going to be away?'

'Three or four days I should think. Look sweetie, why don't we treat ourselves to a dinner out before he gets back? A whole night of girl's talk.'

'I'd like that very much.'

'Good. We'll go to that little Italian around the corner. You can't make it tomorrow, I can't do Thursday, so Friday night, is that all right with you?'

'Great.'

'I look forward to it.'

Chapter Four

'COME IN,' PAMELA said kissing Karen on both cheeks.

'No maid today.'

Pamela smiled. 'No. I miss him sometimes. He can be very useful.'

It was a beautiful evening. The sky was blue and the sun that had been shining all day had sent the temperature up into the low eighties.

Pamela led the way through the house to the terrace. 'I'm drinking champagne again,' she said. 'It's a bit of a weakness of mine. Would you like a glass?'

'Lovely, thank you.'

The French windows on to the small terrace at the back of the house were open and a bottle of champagne was sitting in the silver wine cooler on a circular cast iron table. Two comfortable-looking white loungers with thickly padded blue cushions had been placed alongside it.

'Sit down, make yourself comfortable,' Pamela said as she poured the champagne. She was wearing a loose fitting black tracksuit and flat-heeled slippers, with her red hair tied up in a neat bun on the top of her head, stretching the skin of her face and making her look rather severe.

Karen sat down and put her feet up on the lounger. The terrace was in shade and was deliciously cool.

'This was all rather a surprise,' she said. 'You're going to have to tell me what I'm supposed to do.'

Pamela handed her a glass. 'Cheers,' she said.

'Cheers,' Karen reprised.

Pamela sat on the edge of the other lounger with her elbows on her knees. 'You can do as much or as little as you like really,' she said. 'This guy is one of my regulars. He's been coming to me for a couple of years. A few times before he's asked me if I could provide a girl who would join me. Just to watch. But if you want to do more . . .'

'More?'

'Well it looked like you were pretty turned on last time you were here. He's at your disposal. He's not exactly in a position to object.'

Karen felt a pulse of excitement in the pit of her stomach. 'Really?' she said.

'Really,' Pamela replied. 'But listen Karen, don't think I mind whatever you do. I'm not forcing you into anything. It's entirely up to you. Take it at your own pace.'

'Is he up there now?'

'Yes. Most of them like to be left alone for a while to contemplate their fate.'

'Do you want me to wear anything special?'

'That's up to you too. I've got some stuff that might fit. Do you want to go up and have a look?'

'Yes. I'd never even worn stockings until a week or so ago.'

Pamela refilled their glasses and they took them upstairs to her bedroom, passing the locked black door at the end of the hall.

'I know,' she said, opening her wardrobe. 'Try this.'

She took out a little pink tube dress, made from a shiny elasticated material. 'It's always been too small for me.'

Karen took a large swig of champagne, then unbuttoned the cream blouse she was wearing, and stepped out of her short black skirt. She saw Pamela examining her rather dowdy grey cotton panties and bra and picked up the dress.

'Better take your bra off too,' Pamela said.

A little shyly Karen reached behind her back and unclipped it. She pulled the straps off her shoulders with one hand while she held the cups to her breasts with the other, before she let the whole thing fall away.

'Mmm . . . you're pretty,' Pamela said.

There was no point in false modesty, Karen thought. In for a penny in for a pound. She hooked her thumbs into the waistband of her knickers and drew those down to her ankles. 'These are surplus to requirements too,' she said, trying to sound casual about it.

She took hold of the dress and pulled it over her head, smoothing the material over her body. It clung to her like a second skin. The hem covered no more than three or four inches of her thighs.

'That looks really slutty,' Pamela said. 'Here . . .' She extracted a cellophane packet of hold-up stockings from the drawer. 'Try these too.'

Karen sat on the bed and drew the stockings up her long legs one by one. There was a sticky elasticated band at the top on the inside of a wide lacy welt which gripped her thigh firmly. The stockings were a buff colour. She got to her feet. The skirt of the dress just hid the stocking tops.

There was a mirror on the wall and Karen gazed at herself in it. She was amazed at the difference the dress made. Her breasts had been forced into a deep cleavage by the tube of tight material that covered them and her legs looked smooth and glossy in the sheer nylon.

'What size shoe are you?' Pamela asked.

'Six.'

'I'm seven and a half, but these might fit.'

She pulled out a pair of red leather shoes with tapering heels that looked as if they were made from glass. Karen tried them on. They were a little too big but would be perfectly comfortable for what they had in mind.

'You look great.' Pamela was staring at her appreciatively. Did her stare linger just a little too long? She picked up a bottle of scent from her dressing table. 'Try this.' she said. 'Chanel No. 19'

Karen dabbed the scent behind her ears and between her breasts.

'Here too,' Pamela said, her fingers briefly touching Karen's stocking-sheathed thighs.

Karen dabbed some between her legs.

'That suits you,' Pamela said, inhaling deeply. 'Now you have to have a name. Something exotic. How about Natasha?' She pronounced the word with a Russian accent.

'Mmm . . . I like that. What about you?' Karen asked, brushing out her hair with her fingers.

'Oh, I'm ready,' Pamela said. She stripped the tracksuit off. Underneath she was wearing one of the most *outré* garments Karen had ever seen. It consisted of a series of black leather straps. They descended from her shoulders and around her huge round breasts, looping into a large metal ring on her stomach. From this ring more straps followed the line of her pelvis down between her legs, passing either side of her labia without actually hiding it, then joining together as they emerged from the cleft of her buttocks, and linking into another strap that passed around her waist. The straps between her legs were tight and squeezed her labia outward so they seemed bigger and more prominent. Each of her rather small nipples had been circled by a noose of black thread, making them seem larger too. Hanging from the thread was a silver chain.

'Just these,' she said, sitting on the bed and indicating the soft black leather thigh boots that had obviously been taken off just before Karen arrived. Pamela eased the boots up her long and meaty legs. They fitted like gloves, clinging to her flesh. A strap set into the leather at the top fastened around the middle of her thigh to keep them in place. Naturally the heels of the boots were at least five inches, tapering to a sharp point.

'Are you ready then?' Pamela asked, finishing off her champagne.

Karen felt her heart beating like a bird trapped in a cage. The sight of Pamela's magnificent body so blatantly and obscenely displayed cranked her excitement even higher. She drained her champagne glass, her hand trembling slightly. She was glad she had been so busy during the day that she hadn't had any time to think about the implications of what she had agreed to do tonight, or what had happened last night for that matter.

Watching the tape with Barbara had made her even more curious about her own sexuality. There was also no doubt it had turned her on. When she had got into bed she had tried not to masturbate because she didn't want Barbara to hear her, but in the end it had proved impossible to resist. Her sex had simply refused to rest, her whole vulva squirming ceaselessly, constantly drawing attention to itself, until she had stuffed the handle of her hairbrush into her soaking wet vagina and fingered her clit. It was only a matter of seconds before she was shuddering under the impact of yet another shattering orgasm, her panties stuffed into her mouth and her head pushed under the pillow to try and muffle her anguished cries of pleasure.

There was only one explanation for this sudden rise in her sexual temperature; she had proved that with Roger. Roger was a better than competent lover but he had failed to arouse her at all. It was only when she had recalled the images of what she had seen on the tape and at Pamela's house that her sexual response had ignited. Without that her reaction to Roger, however conscientious he had been, would have been exactly the same as her reaction to the other lovers she had had: muted and modest.

So if she had some sort of proclivity for domination she needed to explore it further. And Pamela had offered her the perfect opportunity. Exploring the deep pulse of excitement that seeing Barbara and Jessica together had ignited was an entirely different matter.

'Yes, I'm ready,' she said, with more certainty than she felt.

'And don't forget, if you want to join in, feel free.'

Pamela led the way along the hall. Karen watched as her big oval buttocks swayed from side to side as she walked in the high heels, the strap of the harness cutting down between them. She felt an emotion that was unmistakably a surge of lust.

Unlocking the door Pamela swung it open. Once again the lights had been turned out and Pamela operated the dimmer switch to bring them up to a pleasant glow. She ushered Karen inside and closed the door behind them.

A long, narrow, low bench had been arranged in the

middle of the room. Laying along its length was a man. He was totally covered in black rubber: tights, a top with long sleeves, gloves and a helmet that covered his face. His body was slender and muscular as far as Karen could tell and he had a flat belly and a broad chest. There were oval holes in the helmet for his mouth and eyes and an opening at the base of his nostrils, but the holes over his eyes were closed by little flaps and a wide leather gag covered his mouth so the only flesh that could be seen on his entire body was the very base of his nose. The outline of a large erection was crushed against his belly.

The bench was almost the same width as his body and he was tied to it by means of thick leather straps wrapped around his ankles, above and below his knees, his waist, trapping his wrists against his side, and his shoulders. Only his head was comparatively free.

'Comfortable?' Pamela said.

Karen saw the man's head move, turning towards them.

'I've brought a friend of mine to see you. Her name is Natasha. Madam Natasha.' Pamela squatted at the side of his head and unstrapped the gag, pulling it from his mouth. 'What do you say?'

'Thank you, Mistress.'

'You see how well trained he can be?'

'Yes,' Karen said, trying to steady her voice.

'Would you like to see your new mistress?'

The man nodded his head. Pamela folded back the flaps of rubber that covered his eyes. Karen saw him blink then look straight at her. His eyes widened and he stared at her fixedly with an expression she could not read. It seemed to be a mixture of astonishment and fear.

'She's very beautiful isn't she?'

'Yes Mistress.' His voice had suddenly become high pitched and contorted.

'Now I hope you're ready to give me some pleasure.'

'Oh yes, Mistress.'

Karen had a disturbing feeling that, even though she could only see his eyes, she recognised him from somewhere.

'Good. Because my friend Natasha is going to watch everything you do and if she is not satisfied with your performance you will be beaten. Is that understood?'

'Yes, Mistress.'

Pamela straightened up. She winked at Karen then took hold of the front of the rubber tights and pulled them down to the man's thighs, exposing his cock. It sprung up from his belly, reddened by the constriction. It was large and uncircumcised, the foreskin still partly covering the glans, and surrounded by a thick mat of curly black hair. Pamela took hold of it and squeezed it, pulling it into a vertical position.

'Not a bad specimen, is he?'

She dropped the erection then slapped it hard with the palm of her hand.

Karen noticed that the man's eyes had not left her for a moment. Since the bench was quite low she was sure he would be able to see up under her skirt.

Pamela walked over to the wooden cabinet, opened one of the doors and took out a condom and a riding crop. She tucked the crop under her arm and strode back to the bench. Tearing the packet open she extracted the little oval of pink rubber and rolled it expertly over the man's erection.

'Now I think it's time I had some fun,' she said. She tapped the flat loop of leather at the end of the riding crop against his balls, which due to the fact that his thighs were bound so closely together were sitting up on top of them. Then she raised the crop and smacked it down hard on top of the man's rubber-covered thighs. He moaned.

'Be quiet,' Pamela snapped.

Pamela roamed his body, slapping it with the crop. She slapped his chest, the top of his arms and the soles of his feet. Each stroke was hard enough to produce a thwack that reverberated across the room.

The man tried to suppress his cries of pain but it was impossible. By the time she reached his feet he was moaning loudly and struggling against his bondage. But every stroke had made his erection swell and grow even harder.

With the crop still in her hand Pamela stood by his head.

'Can you see me?'

Karen saw his eyes move from her to Pamela.

'Yes, Mistress.'

'You know what I want don't you?'

'Yes, Mistress.' His voice still appeared strained and falsetto.

'Good. I'm not like other mistresses you've had, am I? You know that I do this because it gives me pleasure. It's what I need. It's what I want.'

Pamela straddled the low bench, facing his feet, her sex poised directly above his face, then lowered herself on to him. Karen could see from the expression on her face that what she had said was true. Her mouth was slack and her eyes sparkled with excitement.

Immediately the man reached up and buried his tongue into her labia. Pamela moaned softly as it butted against her clitoris. She turned and looked straight at Karen. It was a look that was unmistakable. It was lust, the same lust Karen had felt in the hallway.

'Harder,' Pamela said in an entirely different tone, smacking the crop down on the man's hip.

The man raised his head, pressing his lips against her labia as his tongue continued to work on her clit. Karen saw Pamela shudder and give an almost imperceptible moan of pleasure, her lips parting slightly and her eyes closed.

She opened them again and stepped away from the man.

'You're going to have to do a lot better than that.'

She turned around and straddled the bench, this time facing his head. She inched herself backward on the high heels until the man's erection was between her thighs, then seized it with her hand and directed it up between her labia.

'Remember you do not have permission to come. Do you understand that?'

'Please Mistress . . .'

'Do you understand that?' she barked.

'Yes, Mistress.'

Karen saw the pink phallus parting the shaved flesh of Pamela's sex, the leather straps on either side of them pushing her labia inward. She used it for a moment to stroke the whole length of her vulva, then brushed it against her clit. She dropped the crop and stretched her other hand up his body. Briefly tweaking his nipples through the rubber she got to his mouth and pushed two fingers between his lips.

'Suck them,' she ordered.

The man did as he was told, closing his lips around her fingers and sucking them in. Karen saw Pamela's body shudder.

'That's enough,' she said, pulling her fingers away. They were wet with his saliva. It dripped on to the black rubber.

Suddenly she dropped herself on to his cock, allowing it to thrust up into her vagina. She rolled her hips, grinding her clitoris against his pubic bone and gave a little cry of delight through her clenched teeth. To get him even deeper she sat on his body and raised her feet off the ground, then rocked herself back and forth.

Karen watched with total fascination. The little pulses of pleasure had hardened into a deep and regular throbbing, her clitoris alive with feeling. It was the same reaction she had had before. She did not understand why the sight of a woman being completely and absolutely in control of a man should be so exciting to her, but there was no question that it was. The man was powerless, unable to do anything but lie there and suffer whatever Pamela wanted to do to him, totally unable to assert his own will.

But it was not only Pamela who had the power over him now. She had invited Karen to do anything she wanted. The experiment continued. There was no need for her to go home tonight with the burning need to masturbate. She could give the handle of her hairbrush a rest.

'I think we should see if he's capable of doing two things at once,' she said, trying the same authoritative tone of voice that Pamela used.

'What a good idea,' Pamela agreed.

Karen walked up to the top of the bench and looked down into the man's eyes. She knew he would be able to see up under her skirt to the lacy welts of the stockings and the slit of her sex.

'Did I give you permission to look at me?' she said, imitating the sorts of things she had heard Pamela and Barbara say.

'No, Mistress Natasha.' The man immediately averted his eyes, turning his head to one side.

Karen wriggled the tight skirt up over her hips, then straddled the man's head just as Pamela had done.

'Come on, get on with it,' she said testily as she lowered herself on to him, the words making her shiver with excitement.

The man turned his head and pushed his lips up against her labia. His tongue burrowed inward and found the mouth of her vagina. It pushed inside.

Karen felt an intense shock of pleasure sweep over her. It was so strong that for a moment she thought she was going to come, her body overwhelmed with feeling. Her eyes roamed Pamela's magnificent body so overtly displayed by the leather harness, her big breasts framed by the black leather straps, the silver chain looped across between her nipples, and her thighs, banded by the black leather thigh boots, spread apart to reveal her sex, her labia forced apart by the breadth of the man's cock.

She managed to pull herself back from the brink. 'Now my clit,' she ordered, relishing the power she had been given.

Immediately the man's tongue moved to her clit. It was hot and wet and she gasped as it nudged against the little button of flesh. He tapped the tip of his tongue against it then began circling it with a slow sinuous movement.

A whole new set of feelings swamped her. She settled down on him, feeling his nose pushing her labia apart and his hot breath playing against the entrance to her vagina. She was so wet her juices ran down the cheeks of his face. She was in total control she told herself. She could pull herself off him whenever she chose or grind down on him harder.

'Oh God!' Her orgasm exploded, concentrated on the point where the man's tongue dallied with her clit but flashing through every nerve of her body, rolling up to her head, the last and most intense flash of sensation right behind her eyeballs, forcing her eyes closed.

When she opened them again Pamela was looking at her with an indulgent smile, but she did not say anything. Instead she began her own rhythm, riding up and down on the man's cock. She did not move far, no more than an inch or two, just pulling herself up slightly then grinding herself back down.

Karen watched as Pamela's body subtly changed, the muscles hardening, her breath shortening, her eyes getting narrower. Far from being enervated by her orgasm she still felt needy, and the extraordinary thing was that watching Pamela's body wind itself up to a climax was having an equally strong effect on her.

The man's tongue was flagging against her clit.

'Don't stop,' she snapped, slapping her hand down on his arm. She wondered what it would be like to turn him over and apply a cane to his buttocks. That thought gave her another sharp of pang of excitement.

The tongue resumed its work. Karen felt her nerves tingling, a profound throbbing tempo re-establishing itself. She reached up to the front of the tube dress and pulled the tight material down over her breasts, then grasped her nipples, pinching them between her fingertips.

She saw the redhead's eyes looking at them with undisguised lust. Perhaps it was what finally tipped Pamela over the edge, because at exactly that moment she threw her head back, dropped her entire weight down on the man and came, crying out ecstatically as her whole body trembled. The sounds and the sight of this was enough to set Karen off too. As the man's tongue laboured relentlessly at her clit she let go of her nipples and her orgasm swept over her, just as intensely as the first. She struggled to keep her eyes open, wanting to watch Pamela for as long as she could, but as the orgasm rose in her like a tide, her eyes were forced closed again.

For a long moment neither of them did anything, half-standing, half-squatting on the black rubber tube of the man's body. Then Pamela raised her hand, stroked it against Karen's cheek and smiled. Nothing was said. The gesture was all that was necessary. She knew Karen had crossed a threshold and would probably never be the same again.

The two women stepped away from the bench. Pamela picked up the gag from the floor. It was a wide strip of leather to which a rubber ball had been attached. She came back to the bench and crammed it into the man's mouth, strapping it tightly around his head. She then pulled the little rubber flaps down across his eyes.

'What are you going to do now?' Karen asked, finding it a little difficult to concentrate on anything but the feelings that still churned up all her nerves.

'Very little,' Pamela said. She stooped to pick up the crop, then touched the leather loop at its end against the man's cock. It was glistening with her juices. They had run down over his balls and were smeared against his thighs. 'I give you permission,' she said. She slapped the loop of leather down lightly against his shaft. His cock sprung up from his belly. 'One,' she intoned, slapping the crop down again. 'Two.' And again. 'Three.'

On the third stroke Karen saw him straining against the bonds that held him so tightly. He raised his head, as if trying to look down along his body to his cock which twitched and throbbed violently. The man cried out, though the gag muffled the sound, and the top of the condom ballooned out, filling with his spunk. After a long minute he allowed his head to drop back on to the bench.

Pamela took Karen's arm. 'You go and get us another glass of champagne while I untie him,' she whispered.

'Good idea,' Karen said. She definitely needed a drink.

Karen heard the front door close. It had taken twenty minutes for the man to get dressed and be escorted out.

'Where are you?' Pamela said, from downstairs.

'Up here.' Karen replied. 'In your bedroom.'

She had brought the silver wine cooler up to the bedroom and sat it on one of the bedside chests. She had kicked off her shoes and stripped off the tube dress then pulled away the light summer duvet that covered Pamela's bed, and was now lying in the middle of it. She had decided to keep the hold-up stockings on. The tight elasticated top that banded her thigh made the flesh above feel more sensitive. As she heard Pamela's footsteps mounting the stairs she spread her legs apart, bent them at the knee and began stroking her sex very gently, as if it were a little furry animal. It had never felt so sensitive.

Pamela strode into the room. She stared at Karen's body for a moment, the expression on her face an odd mixture of astonishment, disapproval and desire. 'What are you doing, Karen?' she said, her voice cold and unsympathetic.

'I thought that was pretty obvious,' Karen said, surprised at how calm her voice was. She had made her decision. She knew what she wanted now and exactly how to get it. 'You asked me last time I was here if I was willing to experiment. Well I was then and I am now.'

'What makes you think I'm into women?'

Karen smiled. 'The way you looked at me in there. The way you're looking at me now.'

'Look, don't you think it would be better if we went downstairs?'

'I think it would be better if you got undressed.'

'All right, I admit I'm bisexual, but that doesn't have to involve you.'

Karen ran her tongue along her lower lip. 'I want to taste you.' What had happened in the treatment room had been enough to convince her that her penchant for domination was very real and not a product of an over-active imagination fed by watching Barbara and Pamela. But she had tried to ignore the distinct physical attraction she had felt for both women, hoping perhaps that it would fade away. This evening, however, the excitement generated by the sight of Pamela's near naked body needed to be faced.

'You've never done this before have you?' Pamela said.

'No, never. You'll have to teach me.'

Pamela looked her straight in the eyes, trying to see if she was really sincere. Clearly what she saw there was reassurance enough. She began to unstrap the leather harness. She eased the little nooses of what appeared to be waxed thread away from her nipples and lay the silver chain on the bed as she sat and pulled off the leather boots.

Karen ran her fingers over the silver chain. 'What do they feel like?'

'Do you want to try them?'

Karen nodded.

Pamela knelt on the bed at Karen's side. She opened the black nooses again then took one of Karen's breasts in her hand and centred the noose over it, pulling the thread tight. The feeling of Pamela's hand on her breast produced a huge wave of feeling. The thread bit into the base of her puckered nipple making it feel hard and tight and producing all sorts of tingling trills of sensation. Pamela pulled the silver chain over to her other breast and secured it with the second noose.

'Looks good,' she said.

Karen looked down at her breasts. Her nipples stood out more prominently than they had ever done. They had turned a deep ruby red.

'It makes my nipples feel so sensitive.' She sat up and shook her shoulders from side to side. Her breasts slapped into each other, her nipples stretched by the weight of the chain. 'Lovely,' she said. She immediately hooked her hand around Pamela's neck and brought her lips up to her mouth, kissing her hard. She crushed her mouth into the redhead's and plunged her tongue between her lips. She had never kissed a woman before and was surprised at how different it felt. The mouth was softer and more yielding. Another wave of feeling swept over her. I'm actually kissing a woman, a little voice repeated over and over again in her head, the idea of it being forbidden and taboo only increasing her excitement.

Karen ran her hand down to Pamela's left breast and dug her fingers into it. She had had an urge to do this from the first moment she had seen her naked. It was not a disappointment. The flesh was pliant and incredibly soft and silky. She tweaked Pamela's small but very hard nipple and felt the redhead's body react with a little shudder.

'Slowly,' Pamela said, pushing her back on the bed. 'Take it slowly.' Pamela looked down at her, examining her body anew, but this time with undisguised lust. 'You're beautiful,' she said.

She moved her mouth down to Karen's neck, kissing and sucking at her skin, then over her collarbone. Her hands moulded Karen's breasts together and she sucked them into her mouth one after the other. The tightly bound nipples responded with a sharp pulse of feeling that was routed directly to Karen's clit. She arched her back up off the bed.

'Lovely,' she said.

Pamela's mouth moved lower. Karen spread her legs apart, eager for the first touch of a woman's mouth on her sex. Before seeing that first tape she couldn't remember ever feeling the slightest desire to go to bed with a woman, and yet now, as she felt the wet trail of Pamela's lips and tongue moving over her flat stomach, she had never wanted anything more in her life. Her sex was alive with anticipation.

As Pamela's hot breath panted against the top of her thighs and the redhead's tongue snaked down to the fourchette of her sex, searching for the little swollen bud of her clit, Karen felt a tremendous kick of excitement. The tip of Pamela's tongue burrowed around her clit, then pressed it back against her pubic bone. Instead of pushing it from side to side her tongue established a rhythm by squashing Karen's clit flat then releasing it again, her thick sticky saliva mixing with Karen's own juices.

'Oh yes,' Karen said with surprise and delight. She had never experienced this before. Almost immediately her body responded to the tempo of Pamela's tongue with an equally stirring pulse.

While Pamela's right hand smoothed over Karen's breasts, gently squeezing the firm, supple flesh, her left ran down to Karen's thigh, moving between the tight nylon and the exposed skin.

'It feels so good,' Karen said.

'Mmm . . .' Pamela murmured without moving her tongue away.

Her fingers snaked upward until Karen could feel them pushing into her labia. They found the open mouth of her vagina, sticky with the copious juices of her sex, thrust an inch or two inside, then scissored apart, stretching the tender flesh. At the same time another finger was butting against the ring of her anus. It too was wet. Karen's sphincter resisted momentarily then gave way and Pamela's finger slipped into the tight, hot passage as the other two thrust upward into her vagina.

Karen moaned loudly. This was all so new. She had never allowed a man to penetrate her anus but now the way the two fingers in her sex and the one in her arse grated against each other, separated only by the thin membranes of her body, was driving her mad with pleasure. The throbbing pulse was getting heavier. She knew she was going to come with indecent haste but there was nothing she could do to stop herself.

'Yes, oh God, yes,' she cried, tossing her head from side to side, as she pushed her body down on to Pamela's fingers, wanting them deeper inside her.

Pamela's tongue did not waiver. It pressed Karen's clit back against the underlying bone then relaxed; Karen was sure she could feel the tiny papillae on the surface of the tongue rasping against the little knot of nerves. Her orgasm began deep inside her sex, at the point where the finger right at the top of her vagina and anus seemed to rub against each other, the flesh trapped between them creating extraordinary waves of feeling. The waves spread out like ripples on a pond, reaching her clit first and doubling every sensation it produced. It travelled up to her breasts, and at that moment Pamela, only too aware of what was going on

94

in Karen's body, plucked at the silver chain, pulling it up and causing the little nooses to bite strongly into the flesh of Karen's nipples.

That was the last straw. As she had masturbated hungrily over the last few days, her mind had filled with images of Barbara's and Pamela's naked bodies and the men they tormented so mercilessly. But now, as her orgasm took over her body, racking through every nerve, no images appeared, the sight of Pamela's body, her big breasts quivering slightly, her long legs folded under her, the little strip of hair on her mons just visible, was enough provocation in itself. Karen tried to hold her eyes open for as long as she could, drinking in the vision that knelt at her side, but soon her orgasm produced that sharp hard sensation at the back of her eyes, and her lids were forced closed as she cried out loud and her body arched off the bed like a bow.

As she came down from the high she realised she was whimpering, making little noises of pleasure as her whole body trembled uncontrollably.

Pamela sat up. 'I take it the experiment was a success,' she said with a smile.

'It's not over yet.'

Karen sat up. She kissed Pamela on the mouth, licking up her own juices and savouring them. She tasted good. Then she began to push Pamela back on to the bed.

'You don't have to,' Pamela said.

'I want to,' Karen said.

It was true. She had felt what a woman could do to her, but she needed to reciprocate. She badly wanted to feel Pamela's sex against her lips.

Pamela lay back on the bed as Karen knelt beside her, facing her feet. She moulded the mountainous flesh into two peaks, squeezing Pamela's breasts together, then used her teeth to tweak her small nipples one after the other, while her fingers kneaded the supple flesh. Then, with none of the subtlety Pamela had employed, she dipped her head to Pamela's mons and used her hands to pull her thighs apart.

Without any hesitation she dropped her mouth down on to Pamela's sex, kissing her labia as if they were a mouth, squirming her lips against them while her tongue darted out to lick at her juices. A profound pulse of excitement bounded through her as for the first time in her life she felt the melting softness of a woman's vagina closing around her tongue. Eagerly and hurriedly she moved her tongue up to Pamela's clitoris while she pushed her fingers into her vagina. Imitating what Pamela had done to her she butted the tip of another finger against the little ring of muscles at the entrance to her anus. It was wet from Pamela's own juices and it was not hard to push inside.

The effect of thrusting three fingers deep into the two passages of Pamela's body was almost as pronounced on her as it obviously was on Pamela, whose body shuddered. Karen's own vagina reacted as if it was the one that had been penetrated. The flesh of Pamela's vagina felt like wet velvet, clinging and hot, and it seemed to be rippling with little pulses of sensation.

Her clitoris was throbbing too. Karen pressed her tongue against it, just as Pamela had done to her, then released it. It was large, much larger than her own she thought, and felt rock hard.

'Lovely, darling, that's so lovely,' Pamela said, her hand caressing the curves of Karen's buttocks.

'God, I'm so turned on,' Karen said, and it was true. The orgasms she had experienced seemed to be lingering in her body, keeping her nerves on edge. The tiny nooses tied so tightly around her nipples were provoking her too, and crushed between her legs her labia tingled almost painfully.

Karen knew what she wanted next. Without moving her head away she raised her leg and swung it over Pamela's chest. The redhead responded immediately. She ran her hands over the tops of Karen's thighs and pulled her back towards her, raising her head and planting her mouth firmly on Karen's sex.

Suddenly they were joined. Everything that Karen had felt before paled into insignificance now they were coupled like this. It was as though she had been plugged into an electric current. Her sex erupted, her clitoris squirming wildly against Pamela's tongue as the redhead pressed her mouth into her labia. Everything she did to Pamela, Pamela was doing to her, so everything she felt, every pulse and thrill of feeling, was echoed in Pamela's body, and that, like a vicious circle, only increased her own pleasure.

Within minutes the circle of orgasm was beginning again, this time centred on her clit. But as the little button of nerves began to swell and gyrate, transmitting a huge wave of pleasure, she felt Pamela's clit, hard against her own tongue, behaving in exactly the same way. She could feel from the way Pamela's body was quivering, her pulpy breasts crushed against her belly, her thighs pressing against her cheeks, that Pamela's orgasm was just as close as her own.

They squirmed against each other, wallowing in the sensations they were creating, their tongues working at the same tempo, their fingers renewing their thrusting movements in both passages of their bodies. They came together once, moaning and crying out loud, the noise muffled by their sexes, but this was only a prelude to an even greater climax, the first orgasm driving them on to a second, making them even more sensitised to each other's needs and the driving passions that swamped them both. Without a pause they continued sensuously moulding their bodies together in a single rhythm, the sensations from their soft pliant breasts, shaking and shivering with each movement, in contrast to the sharp, intense excitement from their clits. It went on for a long time, sweat lubricating their bodies to add yet another slippery sensation, both wanting to hold off the final climax until the last possible moment, the prelude to orgasm almost as good as the orgasm itself.

Finally they could hold back no longer, every nerve and sinew stretched by need. And then they came, wholly and completely, their bodies suddenly as rigid as steel, pressed together and totally still while their clits and vaginas writhed uncontrollably, their orgasms wiping away everything but the feeling itself.

Neither moved for a long time.

'Oh Christ, that was amazing,' Karen said, peeling herself off Pamela's body and laying at her side.

'You're very good at it,' Pamela said.

'For a beginner you mean?'

'No. You've got the most marvellous touch Karen. It must be an instinct.'

'It was wonderful. I'm still shaking.'

'So the experiment was a success?'

The question took Karen by surprise. In the heat of sexual excitement, the excitement that had started in the treatment room, she had known perfectly well what she wanted. Seeing Pamela's naked body again had provoked all the feelings she had tried to suppress. But now those feelings were out and in the open, now she could not kid herself for one second that she had not enjoyed and relished the sexual contact, the homosexual contact with another woman, she did not know what consequences that held for her. It was a little frightening.

'Yes,' she said quietly, 'I think you could say that.'

Chapter Five

MALCOLM TRAVERS WAS staring at her from the window of his office on the upstairs landing. Tina noticed it as she delivered a mug of coffee to Karen's desk.

'He fancies you,' she said, glancing backwards towards the gallery.

Karen looked up but the moment their eyes met he turned away.

'No he doesn't. He's happily married.'

'Doesn't mean he wouldn't have a fling. I wouldn't mind going a couple of rounds with him. He's gorgeous. And I'd love to find out what he's got under those beautifully cut trousers.'

'Tina, stop it.'

'Ah well, better go and try and find a vet for Mrs Davenport. Her tortoise needs attention.'

'Good luck.'

The phone on Karen's desk rang.

'Karen, it's Pam.'

'Pam, how are you?'

'I feel great actually. Must be all that good sex.'

Karen felt herself blushing.

'Anyway, I just wanted you to know you were a

great success. He's mad about you. Thinks you're dazzling. Are you interested in another go?'

'What do you mean?'

'Another double-header with me. He'll pay the same rate.'

'Another two hundred!' It had been quite late when she'd left Pamela's house last night. They had both been starving hungry and Pamela had cooked them pasta and salad and produced a selection of cheese. They called for a taxi to take Karen home and at the front door Pamela had given her a sealed white envelope. It contained four fifty-pound notes.

'Yes.'

Four hundred pounds was a lot of money. But she knew it wasn't that which motivated her. 'I'd love to.'

'Great. Monday at seven. Is that all right?'

'What about the weekend?'

Pamela laughed. 'Married men stay home at the weekend. They only come out to play on weekdays.'

Karen hadn't thought about that. 'Monday then.'

'I'll look forward to it,' Pamela said, in a tone that left little doubt that it was not only the man who would be expecting a repeat performance.

'Me too,' Karen said, hoping this was true. She put the phone down. Surprisingly she had slept like a log last night, and if she had had any dreams she certainly hadn't remembered them. She had woken this morning feeling refreshed and renewed but that did not mean that she didn't have all sorts of doubts about what she had done. They nagged at her all the way to work and at quiet moments ever since.

She did not like the idea that she might be a lesbian, she knew that much. She did not want to start looking at other women as sexual objects and going to gay bars to pick them up. But there was no denying what she had felt with Pamela last night. The enormous outpouring of sexual energy was almost like a dam bursting, as if her body had at last found an outlet for years of pent-up emotion.

Of course, it had not only been about Pamela. She hoped that what she felt for Pamela, the almost over-whelming desire she had had to take her to bed, was a product of the extraordinary sexual tension that being with a submissive male had produced. She told herself that right from the beginning the two things had gone together. Watching the video in Barbara's sitting room, the kick of desire she had experienced looking at Barbara's smooth and shaven sex, had only been one part of her response to what she was seeing on screen. And last night it was her reaction to the man, and his total submissiveness, that had initially created the sexual atmosphere which had led her to be so bold and demanding with Pamela.

There was no doubt that the feeling of a woman's body pressed against her own, the softness and sensu-ality of a woman's mouth and the sticky wetness and velvety smoothness of a woman's sex had turned her on. But equally, if she thought of the man in black rubber tied helplessly to the bench, if she remembered the way she had used him, that excited her just as much. And after all, when it came down to it, wasn't the fact that she had found that her sexual pleasure with a man had suddenly elevated itself to a different plane when they were bound and helpless and she was in control just as worrying? There was no doubt in her mind now that like Barbara and Pamela she needed to play the role of a dominatrix to get real pleasure from a man.

But whatever problems she had with both aspects of her new-found sexuality she decided that she mustn't forget the pleasure that it had given her. Her body had come alive. Two weeks ago she had thought of herself as unresponsive and not really interested in the sexual areas of life. How wrong could she be? Since she had seen Barbara and Dan in that first video she had barely thought about anything but sex. And it turned out that far from being undersexed, her body was capable of delivering the most extreme sexual pleasure: it just needed the right stimulus.

In the end, she supposed, she might decide that the pleasure was not worth the risks. She knew she was playing with fire and that inevitably she would get burnt. But at the moment she was enjoying herself too much to want to stop. As Pamela had said at the beginning, it was in the nature of an experiment, and she wasn't in the mood, as yet, to leave the laboratory.

'Hi.'

'Hi, I wasn't expecting you to be home.'

'Neither was I. Conference finished early.'

Dan Milton was sitting on the sofa with a tumbler of whisky in his hand.

'Where's Barbara?' Karen asked. She had had to work late and it was nearly seven-thirty. Then she remembered Barbara had said she was busy on Thursday night.

'Gone to some do. I don't know. Have a drink?'

'No thanks, it's been a long day. I want to take a bath.' Besides, she thought to herself, there was something else she was anxious to do.

Dan waved at her dismissively and took another slug of his drink.

Upstairs Karen stripped off her clothes and climbed into her pink towelling robe. She picked up the little bag she had bought in Boots in her lunch hour and walked along to the bathroom at the end of the hall. The bathroom was large with a big tub and a separate glass shower cubicle. She turned on the mixer taps of the bath, pulled off the robe and stared at herself in the mirror over the wash basin. There was not a sign of what she had been doing last night, apart from the fact that she thought her nipples were slightly larger and more tender than usual, the little thread nooses that had been tied so tightly around them having bruised them. She gazed into her own eyes but could see no sign of what she regarded as a total loss of innocence. She grinned at herself sheepishly; she was certainly not innocent now.

In the bath she lathered herself up then washed the soap away with a big natural sponge. Then she reached for the packet she had brought with her and laid the contents – a can of shaving foam, a man's razor and a jar of moisturising cream – on the shelf that ran around the bath. She squeezed the foam into her hand and, sitting on the edge of the bath, applied it to her mons. Then she razored it away, taking her pubic hair with it. It took two applications of foam and two passes with the razor before all the hair had gone. Standing up, she inspected herself in the big mirror on the wall at the side of the bath. It looked odd, her mons smooth and hairless while she could still see tufts of pubes growing between her legs, but it also excited her.

Shaving her labia was much more difficult. She placed one leg up on the side of the bath and smeared the shaving cream over herself. She gasped as she felt a strong pulse of excitement, her sex still tender from what had happened last night. Her clitoris spasmed and began to swell. The cream was soft and sensuous and felt good against her skin.

Carefully Karen pulled her labia this way and that,

trying to create flat planes for the razor to work on, but each movement also produced a pang of pleasure. Trying to ignore the temptation to rush into her bedroom and get her hairbrush out, Karen worked meticulously, razoring the cream away, rinsing herself off then applying more.

Eventually it was done. She sat in the bath to rinse the rest of the cream away then stood up and inspected herself in the mirror. What she saw produced a sharp pulse of excitement. She ran her hand down over her mons and between her legs. Her sex was silky smooth. It would be a nice surprise for Pamela on Monday night.

Getting out of the bath she dried herself off then applied the moisturiser to her sex, rubbing it in vigorously and making herself gasp again. She could remember how unresponsive her sex had used to be; now it needed only the slightest excuse to explode with sensation. The moisturiser left her skin looking glossy and soft. She put on the robe again, hid the shaving cream and razor behind her other toiletries in the bathroom cabinet and unlocked the bathroom door.

'There you are,' Dan said. He was leaning against the wall outside the door. The tumbler in his hand held more whisky. 'Did you have a nice bath?'

'Lovely,' she said, putting her hand under her hair and shaking it out. She walked down the hall to her bedroom. He followed her.

'There's something I've been meaning to say to you,' he said, sipping his drink.

'What's that?'

Karen walked into her bedroom. He followed her inside and closed the door.

'That I think you're very beautiful. I always have. Very beautiful.' He sat on the edge of the bed.

'I think you'd better go, Dan,' Karen said.

'Go, why? We're just having a nice little chat aren't we?' He put the drink down on the bedside table and began unbuttoning his shirt. 'Look, we're both adults. We both know what we want, why don't we just get on with it?'

'And Barbara?'

'You don't have to worry about her. She understands. She understands a lot better than you'd ever know.'

'Really,' Karen said.

'Oh yes. Come on sweetie, it'll be fun.' He lunged forward, trying to grab the front of Karen's robe but missed, falling on to his knees.

'You'd better go now Dan,' she said. 'I don't want to get cross with you.'

'Oh why not? I think that would be fun too.' His hand snaked out with remarkable speed and grabbed her ankle, holding on to it tightly.

'All right that does it, get out of here,' she said angrily. Dan had never done anything like this before, though two or three times she had caught him eyeing her lasciviously across the dining table.

'You're so beautiful,' he muttered, pulling himself across the carpet until his lips were an inch from her captive toes. He kissed them.

'Stop it,' she said.

'I'll do anything,' he said in an entirely different tone of voice. 'Anything you want, Karen.' She could see that his attitude had changed. If his original intention had been to see whether she was willing to romp around with him in the bed, being prone at her feet had sparked another agenda. He was staring at her feet intently. She had seen that look before. It was exactly how he had appeared on the tape, his submissiveness etched into every line of his face.

106

Suddenly Karen felt a pulse of excitement in response to his demeanour. After all, wasn't this what she wanted from a man? She had seen exactly what he was prepared to do for Barbara. He was a submissive, a slave, as dedicated to obedience as Pamela's client last night.

'You have no idea what I want from a man,' she said in the imperious tone she had tested out last night.

'I can learn,' he said, his voice excited and anxious.

'What about Barbara?'

'Barbara won't mind.'

Karen thought that was probably true. She remembered what Barbara had said about not being jealous, and about Jessica's little circle of friends. She had seen evidence of it herself on the video; Barbara had brought in another woman to share with her husband.

'Stay exactly where you are, do you understand? You are not to move an inch.'

'All right,' he said, letting go of her ankle.

Karen walked out of the bedroom and down the hall. Like everything else that had happened in her life recently this was an unexpected development. She opened the Miltons' bedroom and headed for the bedside table. She took out the metal handcuffs, the gag and the blindfold.

Back in her bedroom Dan was lying exactly where she had left him. She walked past him without saying a word and dropped the equipment on the bed. Sitting beside it she opened the small draw in her own bedside table and took out the glossy hold up stockings she had bought. She pulled them up her long legs until they were perfectly smooth, the tight tops dimpling the soft flesh of her thighs slightly. She found her highest heels, a pair of black leather shoes, and put those on too.

'Take your shirt off then lie on your stomach with your hands behind you,' she said.

Dan looked perplexed. He was staring at the items on the bed, no doubt wondering not only how she knew where to find them, but how she knew of their existence at all. But that did not stop him obeying her commands instantly.

Karen took the handcuffs, knelt at his side and, after a couple of minutes spent working out how to lock them, looped them around his wrists and snapped them shut. She stretched the silk blindfold over his eyes and wrapped the elasticated straps that held it in place over his head.

'Get on your knees,' she said. The words produced a little spasm of excitement in her sex. For the first time, alone and unaided, she was in control.

Dan struggled to obey. With his hands bound behind his back he had to roll on his side first, before pushing up into the kneeling position.

'Open your mouth,' Karen ordered.

He did exactly as he was told. Karen stuffed the gag between his lips. It was the same orange ball gag she had seen on the first tape, with the leather strap running right through the middle of it. She buckled the strap so tight that it bit into his cheeks.

'That's better,' she said.

She turned on her heels and waltzed out of the room without a word. When she'd arrived in London Barbara had shown her around on her first day and asked her to pick whichever of the three guest bedrooms on the first floor that she would like. After that there had been no reason to explore further. There was now.

Karen wandered down the corridor. There were three doors to the right at the front of the house, where the Miltons had the master bedroom, and three on the other side, including her own room and the guest bathroom. She opened the door of each of the guest bedrooms in turn but they revealed nothing untoward. Where then was the 'treatment room', the grey room she had seen on the video?

Was there an attic or a cellar, she wondered, or was it hidden away downstairs? She was just about to go down to look when she noticed a large mirror attached directly to the wall in one corner of the last guest room. For some reason it looked oddly out of place.

Going inside she examined it carefully. One side of the mirror had hinges fitted to the frame, so she gripped it on the opposite side and pulled. The mirror swung open. It had been attached to the frame of a door; on the other side was the grey room.

She examined the room briefly. There was the horizontal bed-like wooden frame and mattress that she had seen in the video, with the straps and leather cuffs at each corner, and the vertical metal frame in the middle of the room. Behind the door there was a chest of drawers, which she soon discovered was stuffed with all manner of equipment. The top drawer contained gags, cuffs, white nylon rope, cock harnesses and leather straps of every thickness and length, as well as tawses, canes and whips and a selection of dildoes and vibrators. The bottom two drawers were stuffed with exotic lingerie, in rubber, leather and PVC. There were bras, basques, and suspender belts, and pants with rubber cylinders projecting out from the front or inward from the crotch.

Karen marched back to her bedroom.

'On your feet,' she said.

Dan managed to struggle to his feet. She could see that a large bulge was distending the front of his trousers.

Karen unbuckled his black leather belt and slipped it out of his trousers. She quickly threaded the tongue of the belt through the buckle again to form a loop which she slipped over his head.

'Follow me,' she said, pulling him by the belt. She led the way into the hall. As they turned into the guest bedroom she could sense his surprise. Despite what she had done to him already he hadn't realised she knew *all* his secrets.

'Barbara told me. She told me all about you,' Karen said, answering his unasked question. It was almost true.

She pulled him over to the vertical frame, standing him in the middle of it.

'Stay there,' she ordered.

She crossed to the chest of drawers and took out a length of white nylon rope. There was a pair of wooden steps in one corner of the room and Karen took them back to the frame, placing them immediately behind Dan. Then she wound one end of the white nylon rope over the central link of the handcuffs, stood on the steps – which she guessed were provided exactly for that purpose – and looped the rope through a metal ring in the middle of the horizontal bar that formed the top of the metal frame. She pulled on the rope, forcing Dan's wrists into the air and making him bend forward. With his body at right angles to his legs, just as Andrew's had been in Pamela's treatment room, she tied the rope off securely to the handcuffs again.

Pushing the steps back, Karen wrapped her arms around his back and undid the front of his trousers. She unzipped his fly then pulled his pants and trousers down from the back.

'That's much better,' she said. She slapped her hand lightly against his hard buttocks. There were several long stripes cutting into the white flesh, some a light pink, others – more recent perhaps – scarlet red and even a dark purple.

Walking around to the front of him she felt her clit give a little spasm of feeling as she saw his cock. Of course she had seen it before on the video but in real life it looked bigger, the network of veins that surrounded it sticking out prominently, like ivy wrapped around the trunk of a tree. It seemed to quiver under her gaze.

Karen was amazed at how calm she felt, and how she had been able to use the situation with Dan to her own ends. He was considerably older than her and a great deal more experienced, but in a matter of minutes she had been able to reduce him to the role she had seen him playing for his wife. She couldn't imagine how she would have reacted to Dan's advances before her experiences with Pamela. She would certainly have been upset, if not scared. Now, it seemed, she could take it in her stride.

Dan tried to say something but the words were muffled on the ball gag.

'Be quiet,' she snapped.

Karen pulled his shoes, socks, trousers and pants off so that he was completely naked. Tentatively she took his cock in her hand. Her body shuddered with excitement. She suddenly remembered Roger and how she had fantasised about tying him to the bed. How would it have felt if he had been completely in her power? She squeezed the phallus and felt it throb in response. She hadn't the faintest idea why this experience excited her so much but there was no question that it did. She could already feel that little tingling sensation in the depths of her vagina that she knew meant her juices had already started to flow.

'Spread your legs apart,' she ordered.

Dan spread his legs as far as he could, but with his arms twisted up behind his back it was not easy. Karen pulled his ankles over to the bottom corners of the frame and strapped them into the leather cuffs that were chained there.

She stepped back to admire her work. It might not have been as expert as the positions she had seen on the video and in Pamela's house, but it was effective. Dan's body was cramped and completely powerless.

'Now let's see,' she said. She was enjoying herself now, the dominatrix *manqué*. Going back to the chest of drawers she took out a tawse, a two-foot strip of thick leather shaped into a handle at one end with the other split into three. She stripped off the pink towelling robe and let it slip to the floor. With her sex newly shaved, still feeling lustrous with the moisturiser, and the glossy black hold-ups sheathing her legs, she had never felt so naked. It was a wonderful sensation.

'I'm sure Barbara would want me to punish you for what you did, aren't you?'

He shook his head vigorously. Sweat was starting to run down his forehead and drip on to the floor. He tried to raise his head to look at her but the strain on his neck muscles was too great and he had to lower it again.

'Oh I'm sure she would. You didn't know I was into this did you, Dan, that I like men to be my slaves?'

He shook his head again.

'Are you a good slave?' She liked that word. It excited her.

He nodded.

'Let's see then shall we?'

She walked behind him. He tried to twist his head back to see what she was going to do but couldn't get it very far.

'Six seems to be the traditional number,' she said.

She raised the tawse and slashed it down on his already marked buttocks. It made a satisfying thwack and his buttocks quivered just as Andrew's had done the first time she'd administered this treatment. Thwack. The tawse did not produce the thin line of the cane but a much broader and less vivid stripe. Thwack.

'Please . . .' he moaned through the gag.

Thwack. Thwack. Thwack. Each stroke was harder and better aimed. And each vibration seemed to travel up Karen's arm and through her body to her sex, her clitoris buzzing.

She threw the tawse aside. Teasingly she ran her hand over his tortured buttocks and was amazed by the heat they were generating. The idea that she could do anything she liked to him and that there was not a single thing he could do to stop her was driving her wild with lust. Placing her hands on her hips she rubbed her belly against his bottom and he moaned loudly through the gag.

Quickly, she unknotted the white nylon rope. His wrists fell back and he straightened up with an audible groan of relief. Karen walked around in front of him and unstrapped the gag. He was staring at her body and she saw his eyes widen as they feasted on her firm, round and proud breasts, her flat belly and her hairless, sleek sex.

'Well,' she said, spreading her legs apart and running one finger down between her labia. 'Won't you just love to fuck me?'

He nodded fervently. The beating she had given him had only increased the size of his cock. It was twitching against his belly and a tear of fluid was dripping from the little slit of his urethra. She leant forward and whipped it away with her finger, a gesture that left his whole body quivering.

In her regular masturbation rituals since she'd seen the first tape she had fantasised about what it would be like to have a man as her slave. Of course, with Pamela, she had experienced the real thing, but in the end what had happened had been under Pamela's control not her own. Now her fantasies had truly turned to reality. For the time being at least, Dan belonged to her. And she knew exactly what she wanted. Her body was telling her in no uncertain terms.

Intensely aware of his eyes following her she walked back to the chest of drawers. She opened the top drawer and took out one of the dildoes, a smooth cream-coloured one with a straight shaft. Without another word she lay down on the horizontal frame immediately opposite Dan, scissored her legs apart and bent them at the knees, arching her buttocks off the bed so he would be able to see the whole plane of her sex. She caressed it with her hand, the unaccustomed smoothness giving her little pangs of pleasure. She allowed her fingers to dally with her clitoris for a moment, then probe the mouth of her vagina. She saw his eyes watching her hungrily, his body straining against his bonds as if trying to get closer to her.

Karen took the dildo in her right hand. She didn't think she had ever needed sex so much in her whole life. Her own appearance was provoking her – the tight black stockings that banded her thighs, her smooth silky vulva – quite as much as Dan's bound and help-less body and his hard cock. She slipped the dildo under her thigh and pushed it straight up into her vagina, the copious flow of her juices allowing it to thrust straight up to the neck of her womb. It was her turn to moan. She tossed her head from right to left as her sex clenched around the hard plastic, as tight as any fist.

This was outrageous she told herself. It was beyond the pale of normal behaviour, but that was what made it so exciting. Besides, as Pamela had said, when it came to sex there was no such thing as normal. She wished she'd discovered that earlier in her life.

Twisting the gnarled knob at the base of the dildo she felt vibrations bound through her body.

She stared at Dan. His eyes were locked on her sex. She could see him bucking the air with his cock, no doubt imagining what it would feel like if she were to allow him to take the place of the plastic dildo. But she had no intention of doing that. Instead she began to frot her clitoris with the middle finger of her left hand, while she pushed the dildo back and forth in her vagina with her right. The dildo filled her a great deal more effectively than the handle of her hairbrush had done, and the vibrations were so strong they reached her clit, making it tingle on the inside to add to the sensations her finger was creating outside.

She was coming. And she knew he could see everything. She had never masturbated in front of a man before but it was not only that which was exciting her. The main motor of her orgasm was as much mental as it was physical. Whatever happened here in this room, she was in control. That was the thought that ultimately made her sex contract around the plastic phallus, made her clit leap with a sharp pulse of almost unbelievable pleasure, and launched her into an orgasm that took her over completely. She felt as if the whole world was suddenly focused on the tiny space somewhere between the very top of her vagina and the tip of her clit. Though her body was rigid with every muscle locked it felt as if she were floating.

The dildo slipped from her body with a squelching sound. The impact of this, like an orgasm in miniature, seemed to revive her.

She looked across at Dan. He was no longer straining at his bonds and his body was completely relaxed. Then she saw why. Dripping from the end of his rapidly shrinking cock was a sticky fluid. It was spattered in a straight line across the grey carpet, some of it almost reaching the mattress. Dan had been so excited by what he'd seen he'd ejaculated.

'He's going to have to be punished for that.'

Karen looked past Dan to the figure that stood in the doorway. It was Barbara.

'Is this a private party or can anyone join in?' she said.

'So that's everything,' Karen said, picking up her wine glass and sipping at it.

'My God, I had no idea,' Barbara said.

'It was just one of those coincidences. Seeing the tape and meeting Pamela.'

They were in the little Italian restaurant around the corner from the Miltons' house having the dinner they had arranged on Tuesday. They had just eaten spaghetti vongole and misto fritto and were halfway through two large portions of tiramisu.

'So when Dan tried it on . . .'

'I just seemed to slip into the role naturally,' Karen said.

The fact that Barbara had found Karen in the treatment room with her husband had not seemed to bother her in the least. She inspected the way Dan was bound, decided he needed further punishment for daring to come without permission, then taken advantage of the renewed erection this had given him while

Karen watched. It was as though Karen had stepped through the television screen and had become part of the video.

Afterwards it had been too late to talk about what had happened and in the morning Karen had had to rush off to work, so the dinner was her first opportunity to find out what Barbara really thought. She had been eager to explain how her interest in domination and submission had developed since seeing the first tape on the Miltons' video, and had told her all about Pamela, well not quite all, leaving out what had happened in Pamela's bedroom on Wednesday night.

'It's good to be able to talk about it,' Karen said. 'I could hardly tell anyone at work.'

'Yes, that's what I felt when it first happened to me. I thought I was really peculiar. But then I got to know more and more people who were into it. Everyone has got their kinks and quirks.'

'You said there was a group . . .'

'Yes. A year ago I met Jessica. You remember her? The black-haired girl. She introduced us to this little group of women who were all into the same thing. We get together sometimes with our . . .' She lowered her voice, '. . . slaves. Can be quite interesting.'

'And is Jessica the only one you . . . you go to bed with?'

Barbara smiled. 'No. There are one or two others. I go to their houses or they come to mine. It drives Dan wild as you probably noticed on the tape.'

'It drove me wild too,' Karen said quietly. This seemed to be a good moment to broach the subject. 'Look, there's something else I should have told you about Pamela.'

'Go on.'

The waiter appeared before Karen could continue.

'Would you like coffees, Madams?' he said in a heavy Italian accent.

They both nodded and he went away.

'Well, I suppose to be truthful it started with watching that first tape too. I'd never seen a woman naked before, I mean not like that, not so exposed.'

'I know what you mean.'

'And I have to admit it wasn't only the domination that turned me on. I tried to ignore it but I kept having fantasies about being with a woman . . .' Karen shuddered as she thought about it.

'And?'

'I think being dominant, taking control, made it easier for me to express what I really wanted. I was pretty outrageous. We ended up in bed together.'

One of Barbara's eyebrows rose. 'And did you enjoy it?'

Karen looked her straight in the eyes. 'Yes.'

They both knew the implications of that answer but Barbara said nothing. The waiter delivered the coffee.

'Anything else, Madams?'

'I think we both need a brandy,' Barbara said. 'I certainly know I do.'

'But of course.' The waiter hurried away.

'So what do we do now?' Barbara said quietly.

Karen knocked on the door.

'Come in.'

It was Monday morning and when she'd arrived at work there was a note on her desk to say that Malcolm Travers wanted to see her. 'You wanted to see me Mr Travers?'

'Malcolm, please. Yes, sit down won't you.' He was sitting behind his desk in a high-backed tan leather swivel chair. His office was neat and orderly and his desk was uncluttered, with a computer terminal to one side and a single telephone. There were two black leather and chrome chairs in front of the desk and Karen sat in one of them, crossing her legs. She caught him following that movement.

For a moment Malcolm said nothing, staring at her legs with an odd expression on his face, almost as if he were in a trance. Suddenly the spell was broken. 'Oh,' he said. 'Sorry, miles away. I just wanted to tell you that I'd had a call from Mrs Mortimer. She was one of my first customers and she says she's absolutely delighted with what you did for her. She called me personally.'

Karen felt herself blushing. Mrs Mortimer had wanted her house redecorated while she was away on holiday. Karen had supervised the job personally and it had all been completed on time.

'The contractors worked very hard.'

'Well, I believe in passing on credit so consider yourself patted on the back. And I think we should end your probationary period. I'm going to put you on full salary as from next Monday.'

'Thank you, that's great.'

'Well, keep up the good work.'

'Thank you Malcolm, I'm really grateful.' She got to her feet.

'Eh Karen, there's one other thing. I just wondered if you would like to have dinner with me one night.'

Karen did not know what to say. She had seen Malcolm's wife in the office several times. She was a beautiful and elegant woman who worked in a public relations company.

'I don't understand,' she said. She had never heard any of the girls in the office mention that Malcolm was a philanderer.

'I hope this won't go any further, but my wife and I

have been having problems for quite some time. I don't think our marriage is going to last much longer. I would really appreciate some feminine company.'

Karen looked him straight in the eyes. Going out with a married man, she knew, was playing with fire, especially a married man as attractive as Malcolm. In normal circumstances she wouldn't have dreamt of it. But the circumstances of her life at the moment were hardly normal and she was in the mood to take risks. Besides, she liked Malcolm and accepting an invitation to dinner didn't mean she was going to end up in bed with him. She could take that decision later.

'I would like that,' she said boldly.

He beamed a smile at her. 'Great. Next week? Wednesday? Can I pick you up about eight, is that all right?'

'Yes, that's fine. I'll look forward to it,' she said.

'I'd appreciate it if you didn't mention it to the rest of the office.'

'I won't. It's our little secret,' she said, turning and walking out of the door.

Chapter Six

KAREN CLIPPED THE white satin waspie around her body. It fitted her tightly, emphasising her narrow waist and leaving her breasts free. She opened the cellophane packet and took out the stockings, sheer white stockings with a fully fashioned heel and a seam. Sitting on the bed she bunched one of the stockings into a pocket then raised her leg and wriggled her foot into it. Slowly she unrolled the sleek glossy nylon, watching as it encased her leg. Satisfied that it was perfectly smooth she clipped it into the long satin suspenders of the waspie at the top and the side of her thigh. She repeated the process with the second stocking.

'Mmm . . . I like that,' Pamela said. 'Very sexy.'

Karen had taken the two hundred pounds Pamela had given her on her last visit and gone shopping on Saturday morning. Most of her purchases had been lingerie but she had bought a pair of shoes too.

'I hoped you'd like it. What about these?' She took the shoes out of the bag. They were white leather with spiky gold heels.

'They look great.'

Pamela was naked apart from a pair of minuscule latex panties, a triangle of material that clung tightly to her sex. She had come to the front door in a silk robe and led Karen up to her bedroom, where the by now traditional bottle of champagne was waiting. After they had both had a glass Karen had stripped off her dress and got out the lingerie she had bought specially for the occasion, while Pamela had taken off her robe.

'What are you going to wear,' Karen asked, finding it hard to take her eyes off the contours of Pamela's voluptuous body.

'This,' Pamela said, taking a garment from the mahogany chest of drawers in the corner of the room. It was a scarlet red PVC basque with black lacing down the front and a platform bra; crescent shapes formed at the top of the corset to fit under the breasts to support but not obscure them. She wrapped it around her body and sat on the bed next to Karen.

'Do me up would you?'

Pamela sucked herself in as Karen fitted the long row of hooks into the eyes on the back of the basque. Pamela's breasts, big globes of sleek buttery flesh, stood out proudly from her chest, her small nipples puckered and hard.

'I love that feeling of constriction,' she said, as the corset tightened around her body. 'I always think all those Victorian women must have been permanently randy.' She clipped a pair of black stockings into the suspenders of the basque after carefully pushing them under the sides of the latex panties.

'I like your pussy like that, by the way,' Pamela said, as she climbed into a pair of ankle boots with an ultra-high heel.

'I think it makes me feel more sensitive,' Karen said, stroking her mons.

'Mmm ... don't tempt me. We've got work to do. Are you ready?'

'How long has he been in there?'

'An hour.'

'And what am I supposed to do?'

'Like before, anything you want.'

'I'd like to be more . . . aggressive.'

'That's fine. In fact he'd probably enjoy that more. He's got used to all my little tricks. There's one thing though.'

'What's that?'

For a fleeting second an expression crossed Pamela's face that Karen did not understand. She looked sheepish and slightly embarrassed.

'He likes to be gagged. It's his thing.'

'You took the gag out last time,' she said.

'I know, but he doesn't like that. I have to give him what he wants some of the time.'

'All right,' Karen said.

They finished their glasses of champagne and Karen caught a glimpse of them both in the mirror. The sight excited her, as if she wasn't excited enough. Pamela was right. The constriction of the waspie, the way the tight suspenders snaked down her legs, and the clinging nylon stockings made her feel incredibly sexy. But it was not only that. Being with Pamela and watching her dress was a big turn-on too. She was intensely aware of her clitoris and her nipples, both already swollen and hard. She would have loved to pull Pamela down on the bed and replay all the new and unaccustomed sensations she had experienced on Wednesday night.

At the same time she was just as excited at the prospect of entering the treatment room. Her experience with Dan had been crucial. For the first time she had acted on her own, with no one to prompt her or tell her what to do. What had happened was entirely of her

123

own devising and, as a result of that she was sure, her orgasm had been as powerful as anything she had felt before. If she had wanted confirmation that being a dominatrix was really part of what Pamela had called her sexual nature, that had been it. The sight of Barbara and Pamela having total control over a man had given her a new dimension of sexual awareness and had rocketed her body out of its sexual complacency; actually performing the role herself had taken her to a whole new level.

Of course, what she was doing in this house with Pamela was prostitution. She was selling sex for money. But she felt no qualms about that. She was here for one reason and one reason only: to enjoy herself. The money was merely an added bonus.

The two women strode down the hall, with Karen in the lead this time. She opened the black door and turned on the lights.

The man was kneeling on the floor in the centre of the room. His hands were fastened behind his back in a pair of leather cuffs joined by a single metal link and there were similar cuffs just above his elbows, so his shoulders were forced back and his chest out. The same black leather cuffs also ringed his ankles and a white nylon rope had been tied from the central link of these to the cuffs at his wrist, making it impossible for him to stand up. He was naked this time apart from a pair of tiny black leather pants and the rubber helmet that had covered his head last time, its eye flaps closed. A gag of smooth black leather covered his mouth. His body was tanned and almost hairless, and he was slender and muscular. She could see the strong muscles of his thighs and arms pulled taut by his bondage.

But it was his nipples that attracted Karen's attention. Attached to each of these were two tiny chromium clips. Hanging from these clips were heavy tear-shaped weights. They dragged the clips down making them bite more deeply into the tender flesh.

'Good evening,' Karen said, the sight of the man creating a sharp pulse of excitement.

'Mistress Natasha is going to deal with you this evening,' Pamela said. 'So make sure you don't let me down.'

The man bowed his head slightly as if to acknowledge their presence.

As Pamela had raised no objection to her taking the lead, Karen did not hesitate to walk right up to the man. She grabbed the back of his head and pushed his face into her belly. The rubber felt hot. She ground her belly against it as she looked around the room trying to work out exactly what she wanted to do with him. Perhaps, she thought glancing at the double bed, she could combine both her pleasures.

Walking around behind him she knelt down and untied the white nylon that joined his wrist cuffs to his ankles.

'Stand up,' she ordered.

With his arms so tightly held behind his back and no way to spread his feet apart it was clearly going to be impossible to obey but he struggled desperately in the attempt.

'Come on,' Pamela snapped, smiling at Karen.

'I thought you said he was well trained,' Karen said. The two women stood on either side of him, took hold of the top of his arms and hauled him to his feet. When they let go he staggered slightly, his muscles cramped from kneeling for so long, but he managed to steady himself and stay on his feet. Karen saw a large bulge growing in the black leather pants. She wrapped her arms around him and pushed her body into his, her

125

breasts ballooning out against his deep chest. She felt his cock hardening rapidly against her belly.

'Does that feel nice?'

He nodded.

'Did I give you permission to have an erection?' She understood the psychological need to make him feel guilty about something over which he had no control, to invent a context for his misbehaviour.

He shook his head.

'What are we going to do with you? I tell you to stand up and you disobey me. Then this,' she stepped back and tapped his cock with her hand. 'I think you need to be taught a lesson, don't you?'

He nodded and she could see his body tremble with excitement at the idea.

Pamela went to the cupboard behind the door and took out a riding crop. She handed it to Karen with a smile.

'I think he should see what he's getting,' Karen said. Tucking the crop under her arm she carefully folded back the little rubber flaps over his eyes. He blinked against the light then stared at her. For the second time she had the feeling that she recognised him but she could still not put a name to that tiny part of his face that was visible. She saw him examining her from head to toe. His erection twitched against the tight leather.

'Bend now,' she ordered.

He bent forward slightly, finding it hard to keep his balance, the heavy weights on his nipples swinging like pendants.

'More,' Karen ordered, putting her hand on his neck and pushing it down until his head was level with his waist. He swayed but managed to stay on his feet, his bound wrists resting just above his bottom.

'That's better.' Karen raised the crop. At the back the

leather pants were no more than a thong of material that appeared from the cleft of his buttocks and rose to join a thin band of leather at his waist. The marks from last week's treatment were still visible, though they had faded to a light pink. She slapped the loop at the end of the riding crop against his naked buttocks lightly then pulled her arm back and cut the crop down with all the force she could muster. He cried out into the gag and shuddered, his buttocks quivering under the impact. A bright red line appeared across the already pink flesh.

Thwack. The crop cut down again. She watched as the leather sliced into the soft flesh, feeling her own excitement grow. She would never have believed she could take pleasure from doing this to a man, but it made her sex tingle with sensation.

Thwack. This stroke was lower, almost cutting into the tops of his thighs and he reared up and nearly lost his balance. Again he managed to steady himself. Three bright weals decorated his buttocks now.

'All right,' Karen said. 'I hope you have learnt your lesson. Now pull those pants down.'

The man hesitated for a moment, then managed to bring his hands around to the right side of his body, and pull the leather waistband down an inch or so. He then moved his hands to the left and did the same thing there. Slowly, alternating from side to side, he managed to get the pants down a little. But the triangle of material was still hooked over his erection at the front and there was no way, bound as he was, he could reach that.

Karen caught hold of the front of the leather, pulled it over his cock and wriggled the pants down to his knees where they fell of their own accord to his ankles.

'I think we'll take these off now,' she said, flicking at one of the nipple weights with her finger.

'They hurt more when they come off than when they're on,' Pamela said.

'How interesting. Is that true?'

The man nodded.

'Let's try then shall we?' Karen grasped the little clips in her fingers. She could see the jaws of the clips were serrated and were deeply buried in the puckered dark brown flesh of his nipples. She opened both of them simultaneously. The man wailed, the sound muted by the gag. His whole body quivered.

'Now rub them,' Pamela suggested.

The man tried to pronounce the word 'no'. Karen rubbed her fingers against his right nipple and he wailed even louder this time, despite the gag.

'I see what you mean.'

Karen transferred her attention to the left nipple. She could see the mark the clip had left. The man's cock jerked up so violently that for a moment she thought he was going to come.

'Now walk over to the bed.'

The man began to waddle towards the bed, unable to take anything but the most diminutive steps. The mattress of the bed was covered with a single black sheet.

'Sit down,' Karen ordered when he reached his objective.

The man turned around and fell rather than sat down. She heard a sharp intake of breath as his tortured buttocks came into contact with the cool sheet.

'Good,' she said. 'That's much better. You see he can be well behaved Pamela.'

'Oh yes, sometimes.'

Karen went to the cupboard and opened one of the drawers. She took out a condom packet. 'Would you do the honours?' she said, handing it to Pamela.

Pamela knelt on the bed. She pushed the man back so he was lying flat, then tore the packet open, extracted the condom and rolled it expertly over his erection. Gripping it firmly at the base of the shaft she held it upright.

Karen looked down. The phallus was visibly twitching in Pamela's hand and it made her sex pulse too. On an impulse, she stroked her hand across Pamela's cheek and kissed her on the mouth. She caught the look of surprise in the man's eyes as she pulled away.

'Get into the middle of the bed,' she ordered.

The man scrambled to obey. With his arms tied so tightly behind his back his upper body was forced up and he looked awkward and uncomfortable. That did not appear to affect his obvious excitement.

Karen knelt on the bed alongside Pamela. She strad-dled the man's body, positioning herself directly over his cock, but as she spread her legs her labia were so wet and sticky they felt as if they had been glued together. They parted reluctantly, her vagina spasming as they finally came unstuck. She settled herself over his cock and looked at Pamela. 'I'm so turned on,' she whispered.

Pamela smiled. She took his cock in her hand again and eased it into Karen's labia, moving it back and forth, then centring it on her vagina. The smooth rubber was hot. Slowly, wanting to savour the moment, Karen lowered herself on the hard, throbbing phallus. It slid into her on the tide of her juices. For a moment she could do nothing. The wave of sensation that flooded over her was so strong she thought she was going to come. Every nerve in her body came alive, burning with pleasure, every sense wallowing in excitement. The sight of Pamela, with her breasts so lewdly exposed and the red PVC basque and black stockings banding her body, the smell of her rich perfume mingled with the more primitive and unmistakable aroma of sex and the feel of her own tight lingerie, all added to her arousal. She reached forward and touched Pamela's breast. Last time they had done this her feelings towards the redhead had been more ambiguous; now she had no such doubts. Pamela took hold of her hand and brought her fingers up to her mouth. With her eyes looking directly into Karen's she sucked on them hard, creating a new wave of sensation. Then she took the hand and placed it back on her breast, pressing the palm against her nipple.

Karen began moving on the man, pulling back ever so slightly then grinding herself down again, spreading her knees further apart so she could get him as deep as he would go.

Pamela began to unstrap the gag from the man's face. Karen thought she saw what looked like a look of anger cross his face, and remembered what Pamela had said about him wanting to be gagged. But as Pamela pulled the gag clear in one smooth movement she swung her thigh over his chest, straddled his face and lowered herself on to his mouth, effectively gagging him again with her sex. Between her legs the tiny black leather panties were no more than a thong of leather that cut deeply into her labia. Without being told to do so the man immediately tried to winkle the thong out so he could get his tongue underneath it.

Seeing what he was doing was further provocation for Karen. She felt her own clit pulse just as if it were the object of his intentions. She leant forward and touched her lips against Pamela's mouth, brushing them lightly from side to side, then kissing her passionately, mashing their mouths together. She felt Pamela's tongue pushing out against her own and the two danced together, hot and wet.

Without breaking the kiss Pamela moved her right hand down over Karen's breast, briefly tweaking at her nipples, to her belly. She butted a single finger into her labia, stretched open by the man's phallus, and tapped it against Karen's clit. This produced such a surge of sensation that Karen cried out loud, the sound muffled against Pamela's mouth. The finger then began to draw tiny circles on the little button of nerves, at the same time pressing it back against the pubic bone.

'Wonderful,' Karen said. And it was. The combination of the man's hard phallus riding up inside her and Pamela's artful finger was producing the most amazing sensations. They were increased by Pamela's other hand, which began to play at her breasts, one after the other, pinching her nipples then paddling and kneading at the firm flesh. Both touches were perfect, coaxing, cajoling and caressing the feelings out of her. 'You're making me come,' Karen breathed.

'Good.'

The waves of pleasure began to overwhelm her. She forced herself down on the large phallus, wanting to get the maximum penetration, then abandoned herself to the myriad of feelings that were coursing through her body. This was the best of all possible worlds, the hardness of a man combined with the softness and artfulness of a woman's touch. It was not only that of course. The man's total submissiveness, his unquestioning obedience, had turned her on too.

'Oh God, Pamela,' she muttered, as her vagina and clit seemed to fuse together to produce one single surge of feeling that flashed through her body like a arc of electricity, burning everything it touched. Her eyes fluttered and she threw her head back, her body trembling uncontrollably. She let out a cry, a strange vibrato sound that seemed to carry on for a long, long time.

As her orgasm ebbed away she pulled herself off the man and crawled across the bed to Pamela.

'Your turn,' she said.

She moved behind the redhead, crushed her breasts into her back, and sunk her teeth into her neck. Pamela's body quivered. Karen ran her hands around to her breasts and crushed them both back against her rib cage. Then she moved one hand down Pamela's back, over the shiny PVC to the cleft of her buttocks. She found the mouth of her vagina, then, with no hesitation, thrust two fingers deep into her soaking wet sex.

Pamela moaned. 'Lovely,' she said, thrusting her head back so she was just able to kiss Karen on the side of the mouth.

'Is this what you want?' Karen asked.

'Yes, yes.'

Karen prodded a finger against Pamela's anus. The little ring of muscles resisted momentarily then gave way, and her finger slid into the tight, hot passage. With her other fingers already embedded in Pamela's vagina she began sawing all three of them in and out together. The effect the man's tongue was having was only too obvious; she could feel Pamela's sex rippling to the rhythm he had established.

As Karen's left hand ploughed into both passages of the redhead's body, her right pinched at her nipples, using her fingernails to bite deeply into the delicate flesh, and hearing the little moans of delight each pinch created. Pamela's whole body was quivering now, and Karen could feel the waves of excitement that coursed through it.

Suddenly Pamela bent forward. She gripped the man's rubber-sheathed cock in her hand and fed it into her mouth, sucking on it greedily, her big breasts brushing his belly.

It was the man's turn to moan. Karen felt his hot breath expelled against Pamela's sex. Pamela began to pump her mouth up and down, with the same rhythm Karen was using to plunge her fingers in and out of her sex and her anus. In seconds Karen felt Pamela's vagina tense, the velvety walls closing in on her fingers, and her labia flutter. Then her whole body went rigid, she stopped moving and let out what would have been a shriek if the sound had not been muted against the man's erection.

Slowly Karen saw the stiffness in the redhead's sinews disappear. As she slid her fingers out of Pamela's body she saw her beginning to move her mouth again, pushing it down on the man's phallus until it was buried in her throat, at the same time lifting her sex from his mouth slightly.

Karen decided she wanted to share in that too. Coming around to the man's side she leant forward and pressed her mouth to his thigh, no more than an inch away from Pamela's lips. As Pamela pulled back, Karen closed in and sucked on one of the man's balls. She felt his whole penis pulse. She moved her lips up to his shaft and began licking the lower half, while Pamela sucked on his glans. Then they worked together, sliding their lips up and down on either side of his shaft.

The man pushed his phallus up to meet them, arching his buttocks off the bed, his body stretched taut. With his weight crushed into his tightly bound arms the cramp in his muscles must have been extreme, but it clearly only served to increase his excitement.

His cock began to convulse. Pamela quickly moved her mouth over the top of it, covering his glans, while

Karen sucked on his balls again, managing to get his whole scrotum into her mouth. His cock kicked violently and thick spunk jetted out into the condom. He sighed loudly and relaxed, letting his body fall back on to the bed.

'Quite a performance,' Karen said.

'He certainly got his money's worth,' Pamela said.

She reached across the man's rapidly flagging cock and kissed Karen on the lips. 'That was really something,' she said. She looked like she meant it.

Karen sat in front of the dressing table mirror putting the final touches to her make-up. She was wearing the new short black satin and lace slip and matching bra, suspender belt and panties she had bought with the second two hundred pounds from Pamela. The suspenders were clipped into stockings, ultra-sheer flesh-coloured stockings. Behind her, on the bed, she had laid out the new sleek black cocktail dress that she had bought especially for her dinner with Malcolm that night. It was tight fitting, with long sleeves, and a low plunge front neckline.

It had been a busy week at work but quiet at home. The Miltons had gone away for the weekend leaving Karen alone in the house, and though she'd half expected a call from Pamela inviting her round it had not come. She was not sorry about that, however. Everything had happened so fast she was glad of the opportunity to be on her own and take stock of her feelings. She had even resisted the temptation to take out one of the Miltons' tapes, despite the fact that Barbara had made it clear she did not mind, and had even shown her where they were hidden.

Not that she had any regrets. She was very clear about that. She would not have changed a thing. The coincidence of watching the tapes and meeting Pamela in the space of a week had catapulted her into the totally astounding revelation that sex was not just a physical thing, relying purely on the way the various erogenous zones of the body were stimulated, but required complex psychological imagery too, in her case domination and submission. Of course, part of what she had felt was directed at women, but since, in the interim, she had not once felt the slightest flash of desire for any of the extremely attractive women who worked in or called at the office, she was sure that her bisexuality was a product of, and not an addition to, the extraordinary blossoming of her sexuality. What had turned her on so graphically was the idea of being a dominatrix, of reducing a man to the level of a totally submissive slave. This, she was convinced, had produced such an intense sexual reaction in her that it had spilled over, like liquid running from a cup, to create a passion for the two women who happened to be close at hand: Barbara and Pamela. What's more, she did not have fantasies about taking either of them to bed on her own. Having broken the ice once with Pamela she now thought of her bisexuality as a means to an end; another way of torturing and teasing her male slaves.

That was where the problem lay, however. Considering that this was such a drastic departure from what she had thought of as normal sex she was remarkably sanguine about her new proclivities. But the trouble was her future relationships with men. She could not imagine Roger, for instance, allowing himself to be tied to the bed and whipped. Most men, she was sure, would run a mile. No doubt Barbara would allow her an occasional evening with Dan, and Pamela might invite her back from time to time, but that was hardly going to satisfy her on a permanent basis.

She supposed she was going to have to accept that from now on she would have to run a sort of double life, with 'normal' boyfriends indulging in normal sex, and more turbulent encounters with men that Barbara and Pamela introduced her to.

She glanced at her watch. Malcolm was due in ten minutes. Finishing off her eye-liner she got to her feet, climbed into the dress and her black high heels and brushed out her long blonde hair. She hadn't thought much about this evening. There was no question that her recent discoveries about herself had had an effect on the rest of her life too. She felt much more at ease and much more confident. Perhaps the image of an attractive man like Dan willing to grovel at her feet, ready to do her bidding, had changed her idea of her own self-worth. Or perhaps it was just that the total sexual gratification she had achieved for the first time had left her feeling more able to cope with the vagaries of the rest of her life. Whatever the cause, there was no doubt in her mind that it was recent events that had led her to accept his invitation. More than that, they had given her the self-assurance to deal with whatever the evening might hold.

If Malcolm was genuinely having trouble with his marriage she guessed she would be happy to listen to his problems over a good dinner, pat him on the cheek and let him take her home. On the other hand, if his sole reason for asking her out was to try and seduce her she could take that in her stride too. Whether she would agree to the idea she had no idea. It depended entirely on how the mood took her. She smiled to herself. Perhaps she should order him to get on his knees and kiss her feet, see what effect that had on his ardour.

His car pulled up outside at exactly eight o'clock.

'I'm off now,' she called to Barbara, who was working in the kitchen.

'Have a good time,' she answered without coming out.

As she walked down the steps Malcolm opened the passenger door of his large Mercedes.

'You look lovely,' he said.

'Thank you.' She climbed inside the car, inhaling the strong smell of the leather upholstery. He got in beside her and started the engine.

'Where are we going?' she asked.

'A little French restaurant,' he said, pulling the car out into the road.

One where he didn't take his wife, she thought.

'I'm really glad you agreed to come. I know it's difficult for you,' he said.

'No it's not. I'm good at secrets.' That was especially true now.

They fell into talking about the job, and an awkward customer that they had both dealt with who had demanded the refund of her fees because, though the cleaners, dog kennels and chauffeur-driven limousines had all arrived on time and performed their services perfectly, he maintained that they were all late and had done nothing at all.

The 'little French restaurant' turned out to be a grand saloon in a Park Lane hotel. Malcolm allowed the car to be valet parked and led the way through the marble foyer to the dining room, where the waiters were all dressed in tails and the tables were decked out with crisp pink linen table clothes, sparkling silverware and crystal glasses. A little posy of orchids sat in the middle of each table.

The *maitre d'*, a stern looking man who reminded Karen of Christopher Lee, led them to a table in the corner.

'Something to drink?' he asked lugubriously.

'Champagne, I think, don't you?' Malcolm said.

Karen nodded. She hoped that her response to champagne had not yet become a conditioned reflex or her sex would begin to throb. That thought made her smile.

'What are you smiling at?' he asked.

'Just thinking of the last time I had champagne.'

'When was that?'

'Actually it was with someone you know. Pamela Stern.'

'Yes. How is she?'

'She invited me around for dinner to thank me for the work I'd done.' That was another secret she intended to keep.

'That was nice of her. She's a very beautiful woman don't you think.' He said it with surprising earnest.

'Yes I do as a matter of fact.'

The champagne arrived in tall flutes and they talked about the large menu of French food, deciding in the end on the *maitre d*'s recommendations of foie gras, followed by grilled sea bass with beurre blanc. Malcolm ordered a Sauternes to go with the pâté and a Chablis to go with the fish.

He was good company, witty and amusing, and it was not until they had demolished a Pithiviers with crème anglais, and ordered coffee that he mentioned his wife.

'Do you think it makes me a bad person, being here with you when I'm married?'

'Not necessarily,' she said. 'I don't know anything about your relationship.'

'My wife is a very focused person. She is very business like about everything she does. Unfortunately that doesn't leave much time for me. We never get to talk. And sex . . . Well, I shouldn't talk to you about that.'

'I don't mind.'

'Sex is a problem isn't it? You're probably too young to know about that, but take it from me it can be a real pain. If your sex life is messed up it's difficult to think of anything else.'

'And yours is?'

'Yes. It's my fault, totally my fault. Look, I shouldn't be telling you this.'

'Go on, I'm interested.'

The waiter brought two tiny cups of espresso coffee. He deposited them on the table without a word.

'Well I have certain . . .' He searched for the right word. '. . . needs. I think everyone has certain things that really turn them on.'

Karen felt herself blushing slightly.

'My wife is not in the least bit interested. She makes love in three positions and that's it. No variations, no games.'

'That's a shame,' Karen said. 'I think sex can involve all sorts of different things.' She certainly wasn't going to go into detail.

'Exactly. That's exactly how I feel. I've tried to bring it up but Rebecca refuses to discuss it.'

'How long has this been going on?'

'Quite some time. And it's not getting any better.'

The long-faced *maitre d'* approached. 'Will there be anything else Mr Travers?' he asked.

'No, just the bill,' Malcolm told him. 'I'd better be taking you home,' he added.

Karen was feeling distinctly coquettish. 'I'm not sure I want to go home yet,' she said, rubbing the tip of her tongue against her upper lip.

Malcolm stared at her. 'Really?'

'Yes, really. Isn't there somewhere we could go?' He was a married man. He could hardly take her to his marital home.

'We could go to my flat . . .'

'Your flat?'

'Yes. I bought a flat as an investment a couple of years ago. I rented it for a year but it's empty now.'

Karen thought about that for a moment. Now she was really living dangerously, but one of the things she had discovered about herself was that taking risks was not always a bad thing.

'All right,' she said. 'I must just go to the loo,' she said, getting to her feet. A waiter rushed over to pull back her chair. Five minutes later she walked back across the restaurant. As she approached the table Malcolm looked up at her. And that's when she recognised his eyes. They had looked up at her like that, with the same mixture of lust and adoration, in Pamela's treatment room, the rest of his face covered in tight black rubber.

Chapter Seven

THEY DROVE IN silence. At first the realisation that the man in Pamela's treatment room was Malcolm Travers had made her angry. It was possible that Pamela had not told him who to expect on the first occasion and had invited her to add spice to the event. But then he had clearly asked Pamela to bring her back the second time. She had been used.

Her anger didn't last long, however. It turned rapidly to an altogether different emotion.

Malcolm's flat was in Princedale Road, not far from the office. He managed to park almost outside and walked around the car to open the passenger door. She did not thank him.

'It's just here,' he said.

The building was a conversion of a large Victorian house. He took out two keys hanging from a small plain key ring and unlocked the front door. They walked up the stairs to the first floor. The second key opened the door to the flat.

'It's a maisonette,' he said.

The flat was expensively decorated and furnished. The large sitting room overlooked the main road and was decorated in shades of yellow, complemented by two or three large impressionistic oil paintings all clearly by the same artist.

Karen looked around but said nothing.

'Would you like a drink? There's champagne in the fridge.' Her silence was obviously making him ill at ease.

She smiled to herself. He had been prepared for this.

'What I want is for you to come over here Malcolm and get on your knees.' She stood with her feet apart pointing at the carpet immediately in front of her.

'What?' he said, looking puzzled.

'There's nothing wrong with your hearing is there?'

'No.'

'Then do it.'

Malcolm walked over to her. He glanced into her eyes but was cowed by the look of total authority he saw there. He bent his head and thudded to his knees.

'That's better. Now kiss my feet.' The words excited her. She felt her clitoris immediately throb with excitement. Malcolm had handed her the opportunity to indulge all her new-found talents.

'You know don't you?' he said quietly.

'If I want you to speak to me, I will say so. If not, you will keep quiet. Is that understood.'

'Yes.'

'Yes, what?' she snapped. 'Surely you know the correct way to address me.'

'Yes, Mistress.'

'Perhaps you should call me Mistress Natasha. Or are you afraid I'll recognise your voice?'

'Look I didn't mean . . .'

'Shut up,' she insisted. 'Tonight you will call me Mistress Karen. Is that understood?'

'Yes, Mistress Karen.'

'If you do not kiss my feet in the next two seconds I am leaving.'

He immediately pressed his lips to the black leather shoes, moving from one to the other.

'That's better,' she said, stepping away from him. 'Now lay on the floor, face down with your hands behind your back and don't move.'

He scrambled into position.

She walked across the room to what was obviously the kitchen. She found a bottle of Moët & Chandon in the fridge. Taking a glass from one of the kitchen cabinets she strode back into the sitting room. Malcolm had not moved an inch.

Karen sat on the large dark yellow sofa. She put the champagne and the glass on the coffee table in front of her then unwound the cage and popped the cork.

'I'm curious,' she said. 'Was it your idea to get me along?'

'No. No. I had no idea Pamela was going to use you. I was astonished. I thought you'd recognise me. I was furious with Pamela, but she thought it was a big joke.'

'And when I didn't recognise you, you asked for me again?'

'Pamela said if you hadn't recognised me the first time it would be perfectly safe. Especially if she kept me gagged so you couldn't recognise my voice. Don't be cross with me. I did it because you were so beautiful. I've never seen anyone so sexy.'

'And your wife?'

'That's what I was saying in the restaurant. She would never agree to doing anything like that. She's absolutely straight. That's why I had to look elsewhere.'

'How long have you been going to Pamela?'

'Two years.'

'And how do you explain the stripes on your arse?'

'My wife isn't interested. I wear pyjamas. Even if I didn't I doubt she'd notice,' he said bitterly.

Karen poured the champagne. She got to her feet and roamed the room.

'So what do you expect me to do with you now?'

'I don't know. I'm sorry Karen, honestly. I didn't mean to . . . I mean you were just so wonderful. I know it was all a new experience for you, but you seemed so . . . confident. I had to see you again.'

'And if I had recognised you? What would you have done then? Is that why you asked me out?'

'No. Yes. I don't know, I really don't. I suppose I wanted to get to know you better, see what you were really like. I had no idea how the evening was going to end.'

'Where's the bedroom?' Karen asked.

'Upstairs, Mistress Karen,' he said in a meek, obedient voice, hoping no doubt that she would forgive him.

'Are you going to do exactly what I tell you?'

'Oh yes, I'll do anything.'

'Go upstairs and take your clothes off. All of them. I want you kneeling with your hands behind your back and your forehead pressed down to the floor. Is that understood?'

'Oh thank you, Mistress Karen.'

'Don't thank me Malcolm. You may regret playing games with me. Go now.'

He scrambled to his feet and practically ran out the door. She heard him thudding up to the bedroom.

She sipped the champagne and looked around the room. The heavy curtains had tiebacks made from braid silk rope. They would come in handy, she thought.

The shock of her discovery had not affected her

ability to find the situation arousing. She thought of last Monday night and how she had used what turned out to be Malcolm's large hard cock and how, on the occasion before that, he had brought her off with his tongue. After two years with Pamela he was an experienced, willing and expert slave. The prospect of being alone with him, and trying out his talents on her own made Karen smile. She gathered up the tiebacks, the champagne and her glass and walked upstairs. There were three doors on the landing and one of them was ajar. She pushed it open.

Malcolm Travers was naked. He was kneeling on the floor with his forehead pressed into the carpet. The bedroom was large, with a big double bed and mostly modern furniture, the wardrobe, chest of drawers and bedside chests all from the same maker, a combination of lacquered wooden panels and chrome metal. The walls were painted a deep red and the carpet was nearly the same colour. The counterpane and the curtains were red too but in a jagged pattern that was mixed with white.

'At least you can do something right,' she said, walking in and closing the door.

Though it had been over a week since she had beaten him there was still pink stripes across his buttocks.

She put the champagne bottle down on the bedside table with her glass, threw the tiebacks on to the bed, and reached behind her back to unzip the dress. She was glad she was wearing her new lingerie. Wriggling the dress down over her hips she hung it over the back of a small button-backed boudoir chair.

'Where are your trousers?' she asked.

'In the bathroom, Mistress Karen,' he said, his voice tremulous.

Karen walked through into the en suite bathroom. It was decorated with small square grey tiles. She saw his clothes hanging from the back of the door and took his belt out of the loops of his trousers. She would have preferred the riding crop, but this would have to do.

'Well Malcolm, I imagine you know what I intend to do to you now.'

'Yes, Mistress Karen.'

'You have to learn not to lie and cheat to get what you want, don't you?'

'Yes, Mistress Karen.'

Karen swung the strap, aiming it for his buttocks. It sliced down on them with a satisfying smack. He gasped. A bright red line appeared intersecting one of the existing red stripes. She held the belt up, this time gripping the end in her other hand, then slashed it down with all her might. He yelped as the leather cut into his flesh. His head reared up reflexively, but he immediately pressed it forward again.

Karen felt the familiar sensations coursing through her body. Her clitoris began to throb and she felt that tingling right at the top of her vagina that was the usual precursor to a flood of juices. She slashed the leather belt down across his buttocks one last time. He yelped again. Three bright stripes burned into his flesh.

'All right, straighten up,' she ordered.

Malcolm obeyed at once. She saw his eyes looking at her body and the elegant black satin and lace lingerie. His cock was already erect, sticking up vertically from the top of his thighs, his glans half-covered by his foreskin.

'Come here,' she said. The tone of her voice was domineering. She had learnt her lesson well.

Knowing better than to make any attempt to get to his feet Malcolm shuffled over on his knees, stopping when his face was a foot in front of the black satin slip that covered her belly.

'Closer,' she said.

He moved forward until she could feel his breath on her stomach. Slowly she began inching the satin slip up her body, the material brushing his face. It rose over her panties, over the waistband of the suspender belt, then revealed the smoothness of her navel. She pulled it over her head then draped the material over him, covering his own head completely, stretching the black satin taut against his face. The satin was impregnated with her perfume – Chanel No. 19, the perfume that Pamela wore – another purchase from the money that it turned out had come from Malcolm.

'Does that feel good?'

'Yes Mistress, wonderful,' he said.

'Suck it.'

She saw his lips grasping at the satin, and he sucked it into his mouth.

'All right, that's enough.' She tired of that game and pulled the slip away. She pushed him lower then edged forward so he was forced to arch his back, his face sliding down between her thighs.

'You know what to do,' she said, her fingers twined in his hair.

Immediately she felt his tongue running along the leg of the panties. He managed to wriggle it under the crotch but the elastic in the legs was too tight for him to get far. She felt him trying to work it up towards her clit but with no success.

'You're useless,' she chided. She used her hand to pull the crotch of the panties over to one side. 'I have to do everything myself.'

Her fingers dug into his hair, pulling his head up again so his mouth was pressed into her sex. This time there was no obstruction. His tongue snaked out between her labia and pushed up to her clit. It tapped against it hard, then flicked it from side to side.

Karen felt such a huge surge of excitement that she gasped. There was no doubt that having Malcolm so completely at her mercy had cranked up her sexual responses. The last time he had done this to her, she remembered, he was strapped to the bench in Pamela's treatment room covered from head to foot in black rubber and completely anonymous. The fact that Pamela's slave had turned out to be her boss only served to add piquancy to the experience.

'Faster,' she said. Malcolm's tongue instantly moved more quickly, flicking her clit from side to side with greater urgency. It was exactly the right rhythm for her. 'Yes, like that, don't stop,' she ordered, her fingers clamped to his skull, holding him exactly where she wanted him.

The initial wave of excitement had hardened into a deep rhythmic pulse that matched the tempo he was using on her clit. She could feel her juices running down her vagina and out over his chin. His back and neck were bent back awkwardly in this position and must have been aching terribly, but she did not care about him. That was the point after all. The only person who mattered, the only pleasure that counted, was hers.

There was a mirror on the wall in front of her and she caught sight of herself, her breasts nestling snuggly in the lacy cups of the bra, the suspender belt and panties banding her waist, the black satin suspenders pulling the welts of the stockings into wide chevrons on her thighs. Malcolm's head, buried between her creamy thighs, moved almost imperceptibly from side to side as his tongue kept up its frantic pace, his hands clasped behind his back as tightly as if they had been bound. The image excited her. It was the perfect symbol of her dominance and his submission.

She felt a new wave of pleasure racing through her body. It would have been easy to control it, to pull herself back from the brink of orgasm, but she had no need to do any such thing. Instead she let the feelings flood over her, staring at herself in the mirror, the reflection creating almost as much arousal as the movement of Malcolm's tongue.

'Oh God . . .' As her orgasm swept over her she swayed, almost losing her balance, eyes fluttering and head thrown back. She steadied herself, let go of Malcolm's head and stepped back. She knew exactly what she wanted now.

'Bring me my champagne,' she said.

Malcolm creaked audibly as he straightened up. He was clearly not sure whether to crawl over to the chest of drawers or walk. He made the wrong choice and started to crawl.

'Quickly you idiot,' Karen barked. 'Get on your feet.' She sat on the little boudoir chair.

Malcolm got up, refilled her glass and brought it over to her.

'Get over to the bed,' she said, her tone as severe as before. 'Strip the duvet off and lie on your back.'

Malcolm scrambled on to the bed and did exactly as he was told. His erection slapped against his belly.

Karen sipped the chilled champagne. The orgasm had left her feeling relaxed and at ease. The shock and anger of her discovery had dissipated and the more she thought about the position she found herself in the more she realised how advantageous it was. She had no idea whether eventually the pleasure and excitement of being a dominatrix would wear thin, or perhaps

149

disappear as quickly as it had appeared in the first place. In the meantime Malcolm was the perfect vehicle with whom to explore and satisfy her every whim. If he wanted to be a slave, she was very happy to take advantage of that situation.

She made no effort to hurry. She took another sip of her champagne and looked at him lying there, staring at the ceiling, not daring to move for fear of incurring her displeasure. That was what made it all so satisfying, she decided. She was in control of the sexual agenda. Before, in her sexual relationships with men, the fumbling uncertainty of it all, of who wanted what done to whom, had irked her. But now all that doubt had been removed. What she wanted was what she got.

Karen got to her feet and went over to the bed. She placed the bottom of the glass on his thigh and trailed it up his body. He quivered, his cock twitching.

'I bet Pamela was very strict with you. But you like that don't you?'

'Yes, Mistress Karen.'

She put the glass down on the table and picked up one of the tiebacks she'd brought from downstairs. She looped it twice around his ankle then pulled his leg outward and knotted it around the leg of the bed. The corded rope cut deeply into his flesh. Following the same procedure with his other ankle and his wrists she soon had him spread-eagled across the bed, his limbs stretched taut just as Dan had been in the first tape she had seen. Though that was only a matter of a few weeks ago it seemed a lifetime.

'That's much better,' she said, as she stood to admire her work. He was looking at her too, his eyes haunted and needy, the bondage obviously creating new cravings.

Karen hooked her thumbs into the waistband of her

150

panties and drew them slowly down her long legs. They rasped against her stockings. She had got into the habit of shaving her sex every couple of days then slathering it with moisturiser and it was smooth and velvety. Reaching behind her back she unclipped her bra, her breasts quivering as they fell from the lacy restraints, her nipples hard and prominent.

Malcolm's eyes roamed her body avidly. Deliberately she leant forward and allowed her left breast to brush against the tip of his cock. It twitched violently. Then she straightened up and ran her hand down between her legs and stroked her labia, allowing her finger to probe the mouth of her vagina. Coating it with the sticky honey of her sex she brought it up to her mouth and sucked on it noisily.

'I taste good, don't I? Do you remember what I taste like Malcolm?'

'Oh yes, Mistress Karen.'

It was incredible to think that she had been talking to him day after day in the office, without knowing he had seen her and touched her so intimately.

'I think you've seen quite enough, don't you?' she said.

'No Mistress, please,' he said.

'What did you say?'

'You're so beautiful, please let me look at you.'

'Listen Malcolm. Let's get one thing very clear. What you want does not matter to me. The only thing I care about is what I want. Do you understand that?'

'Yes, Mistress but . . .'

He had paid Pamela for her services. In the end, Karen supposed, however dominant she was he was her client, and since he was paying the piper she would at least have to play his tune. But that did not apply to her.

'But nothing, Malcolm. Or perhaps you'd prefer it if I went home.'

'No, Mistress, please stay. I'll do anything you say.'

She smiled. Considering the way he was bound he had little choice, she thought. She picked up her panties and stuffed them into his mouth then arranged the black slip over his face. The panties were damp with her juices and he moaned, his body giving a little tremor of excitement.

With his face swathed in black satin he was anonymous again, as he had been before, a body available for her use, with no name and no associations.

Karen's own needs were starting to assert themselves again. Her sex was churning and her clit had swollen so much it seemed to be forcing its way out from the protection of her labia. His body was muscular and powerful, his broad chest and flat abdomen testimony to what was obviously a vigorous exercise regime, and she was sure that seeing it bound so helplessly was adding to her excitement.

'You know you are not allowed to come,' she said sternly, reprising the admonishment she had heard both Barbara and Pamela proclaim.

He nodded.

Kneeling up on the bed, Karen straddled his body just below his waist, her back to his feet. A little thrill ran through her as it always seemed to do when she felt her labia open and the mouth of her vagina part. Tentatively she prodded her finger into her sex once again, wanting to feel the hot, wet flesh. It spasmed as she touched it, as if trying to suck her finger inside.

Reaching behind her back, she grasped his cock firmly in her hand, squeezing it tightly. It throbbed in response. She eased back until it was nuzzling up between her labia and his glans was butted against her clit. Rolling her hips slightly she moved her clit against it, smearing it with her juices.

He moaned.

She leant forward and, suddenly remembering the serrated jaws of the nipple clips, closed her teeth around his right nipple and bit into it, pulling it outward. He moaned again and his cock recoiled against her grip.

'Very sensitive,' she said. His reaction had produced a sympathetic pang in her own nipples. She sent her left hand up to her chest and pinched one after the other, the initial shock of pain turning rapidly to a throbbing, intense pleasure that immediately set her clit throbbing again too.

Her need was too great for any more delay. She pulled his cock back to the mouth of her vagina and dropped on it with all her weight. It thrust into her sex with no resistance, her juices making the penetration frictionless. Grinding herself down on it she felt the smooth glans rubbing against the neck of her womb.

Her physical reaction to this intrusion was another surge of pleasure. She pulled herself up off him until he was poised at the mouth of her vagina, then plunged down again. In this heightened state of sexual aware-ness the orgasm she had just had seemed to spring up anew, instantly reviving all her nerve endings and making them tingle. She lifted herself up once more, feeling the walls of her vagina fold back on themselves, then pushed down more slowly, wanting to feel the big sword of flesh ploughing into every inch of her. But as his glans pressed back up to the neck of her womb, and her whole vagina was wonderfully stretched by the breadth of his phallus, she had another idea. This was her agenda after all. She could do what she liked.

Pulling up off him she allowed his cock to plop out

of her sex, slapping wetly against his belly. She reached behind her once again and took it in her hand.

Hesitantly she pulled it up into the cleft of her buttocks. The shaft was so wet it was slippery and she had to grip it tightly. She centred it on the little circle of her anus.

She had never been buggered, but Pamela's finger had felt delicious as it ploughed into her rear and she had decided it was time to experiment again. Gently she pushed back on the big hard phallus. Her sphincter resisted but then suddenly gave way and his glans lunged into her.

Karen felt a rush of excruciating pain and cried out loud. Even though he was no more than an inch or two inside her he felt enormous, as though he was splitting her apart. But just as the pain from her nipple a few minutes ago had turned to a deep throbbing pleasure, so this new pain did the same. The difference was that the intensity, being so extreme, produced a pleasure on the same frequency, so powerful that for a moment she thought she was going to come, her whole body quivering with a sensation that she had never felt before.

It took her some minutes to regain control of her tortured senses. Then, slowly, she pushed back on him and felt his cock moving upward. Her anus was so sensitive she thought she could actually feel the ridge at the bottom of his glans. With one determined push she ground herself down on him. Again the pain was atrocious, again the pleasure it was transmuted into was so fierce it was like an entirely new experience. It was pleasure and pain together, except the pain had been stripped of everything but its coruscating ability to make every nerve feel raw and exposed.

There was no possibility of postponing her orgasm this time. In fact there was no possibility of doing anything but let the sensations rack over her. She could not move, she could not breathe, all she could do was feel. In the depths of her body, where no man had ever been before, she felt her orgasm kicked into life by the rock hard rod of flesh she was impaled on and then spread outward, the nerves of her body so sensitive they felt as though they had never been used before.

It was a long time before it was over. The first impact, the initial explosion of feeling, was followed by a second and a third, like the aftershocks of an earthquake. Then there were minor tremors and trills, making her body tremble and her sex clench. That was a new experience too. With the phallus jammed into her rear passage her vagina felt entirely different, clutching vigorously at thin air and producing a whole panoply of new sensations.

Eventually she was able to ease herself off Malcolm's cock. She knelt at his side.

She could have left him like that, of course. There was no obligation on her to satisfy his needs. But he had done everything she had asked him to do and she thought he deserved some reward. Besides, this was not the end of their relationship, she was sure. All slaves needed a reward.

Leaning forward she touched the tip of her tongue against his glans. 'You have permission,' she said, mimicking Pamela. Then she sunk her mouth down on his cock, burying him deep in her throat while her hand closed around his scrotum. She sucked on his phallus as hard as she could, then allowed it to slide all the way out of her mouth and all the way back in, her tongue working on the ridge at the bottom of the glans.

It took no more than two or three strokes before she felt his balls contract and his cock spasm. It bucked

155

wildly as she forced it deep again, and hot spunk spattered into her throat, jet after jet of it. She sucked his glans gently to extract the last drops. She had swallowed most of it but some escaped her lips, pearling down her chin and landing on his thigh.

'Thank you, Mistress Karen,' he said, the words muffled on her black panties.

'So what did you say?'

'I told him I'd think about it.'

'It's a great offer. Your own flat.'

'He's going to arrange the mortgage and everything.'

Karen sat in the kitchen with Barbara. She had bought a bottle of chilled champagne in the local off-licence and had opened it as soon as she'd got in, anxious to tell Barbara all her news.

It was a week since her dinner with Malcolm and at five o'clock he'd asked her to go for a drink with him. He needed to talk to her. There was something important he wanted to say. They had gone around the corner to the local wine bar and sat at a discreet corner table. Looking as nervous as a schoolboy sitting his first exam, Malcolm had asked her if she would like to take over his flat in Princedale Road. He would have it put into her name and arrange and pay for a mortgage. In return he would be able to visit her on a regular basis.

'So what brought this on?' Barbara said, knowingly. 'Are you sleeping with him?'

Karen nodded. 'Afraid so,' she said, blushing pink.

'Don't be so sheepish. There's nothing wrong with that.'

Karen had not quite told her the whole story. She had omitted to add that he wanted her to commission a special treatment room in the flat where his new dominatrix could entertain him with all the equipment he had become accustomed to at Pamela's.

'He's married,' Karen admitted, refilling Barbara's glass. She had told Malcolm she would think about his offer and badly needed to discuss it with someone.

'Are you in love with him?' Barbara asked.

'Heavens no.'

'Then that's ideal. If he only wants you for sex, that makes for a nice uncomplicated arrangement.'

'It feels a bit like being a prostitute.'

'Come on. A lot of women sell sex for less than that. I mean, I used to do it for dinner and a bottle of wine. As long as the flat's in your name, even if things turn nasty you're protected.'

'I'd never be able to afford the mortgage payments on my own.'

'Then you can sell up and pocket the difference. Either way you win. I think you should go for it, my love. No question. It's ideal.'

Karen thought this was sensible advice. She had had qualms about accepting the money, even if she was never going to see it directly, but that had not stopped her accepting the four hundred pounds he had given her through Pamela, which was out-and-out prostitution. And, of course, there was another element in the equation. Not only did she get a lovely flat to live in, she was going to be able to exercise her predilections for rather *outré* sex too. She had already made it clear to Malcolm that since he was a married man, she would not be his exclusive property either, and he had accepted that. He would probably not be able to see her more than two or three times a week so the rest of her time would be her own. The arrangement, as Barbara said, was ideal.

*

'Are you busy?' Karen asked.

Malcolm Travers was sitting behind his desk.

'No, come in.' He smiled nervously. Outside in the general office he was still her boss. In the privacy of his office their roles had been reversed.

'Good.'

Karen closed the door and marched in. It was the end of the day and down on the ground floor she could see everyone making preparations to go home.

'I just wanted to tell you that I've decided to accept your offer,' she said, sitting in one of the black and chrome chairs and crossing her legs. She saw his eyes glance down at them. Was he hoping to catch a glimpse of her panties? If so he would be disappointed. She'd taken them off in the toilet a couple of minutes ago. They were stuffed in her handbag at the side of her desk. She had taken her tights off too.

'That's great,' he said. 'I'll get things moving.'

'When can I move in?' she asked.

'Here . . .' He took a set of keys from his desk. 'This is my spare set. There'll be solicitors and stuff like that to have it transferred into your name but as far as I'm concerned you can move in whenever you like. The sooner the better.'

'I'm going to use the carpenter we found for Pamela. Have you spoken to her by the way?'

'Yes. I told her what had happened. She thinks it's wonderful.'

'She's not upset about losing a client?'

Malcolm's face reddened. 'Pamela is very much in demand. She won't have any trouble replacing me. She's like you.'

'Like me?'

'She does it because it turns her on. That's true isn't it? You really get pleasure out of it.'

158

'Talking of which,' Karen said. 'Apparently you're going out with your wife tonight.'

'How did you know that?'

'I asked your secretary. Don't worry I was very discreet.'

'Why did you want to know?'

'Stand up,' she said, the tone of her voice suddenly changing.

'What?'

'You heard.' She got to her feet, went to the office door and locked it.

'Not in the office, Karen.'

'Who made that a rule?' she said. 'You are here to obey me Malcolm, I'd thought I'd made that quite clear.' She was enjoying his discomfort.

Malcolm got to his feet. 'What are you going to do?' he whispered.

'Come around here.'

He started to move around the desk.

'Not like that, you fool. On your knees.'

Glancing anxiously over his shoulder at the window, Malcolm sunk to his knees. Despite his embarrassment it was obvious he found the situation exciting; a bulge was already tenting the front of his trousers.

He was not the only one to feel the excitement. Karen had been planning this for the last hour. She was hungry for sex. It had been over a week now, and after the extremes of passion she had experienced recently her body was not prepared to wait any longer.

She wriggled her short black shirt up over her hips, bent over his desk with her legs spread apart and thrust her bum into the air. She would have never dared contemplate being so blatant in her previous existence, but now she realised exactly how easy it was to get her own way.

159

She looked over her shoulder and saw Malcolm staring directly at her sex. In this position she was sure he could see the whole of her carefully shaved vulva, from the little puckered crater of her anus down to the pink button of her clit, with no hair to obstruct the view.

'Get on with it,' she said sharply.

'What do you want me to do?' he asked, as if in a trance.

'Kiss it.'

He shuffled forward on his knees immediately and pressed his mouth to the long slit of her sex. She felt him explore her vagina with his tongue then move it to her clit. She moaned as he started tapping against it.

'Harder,' she ordered. Before all this had happened to her she had always had to be polite with men, to dress up what she wanted in language intended not to offend, to wheedle around the subject instead of cutting straight to the point. Now she did not have to bother.

His tongue tapped harder, like a tiny hammer.

She looked out of the window and saw Tina glancing up at it. Karen was not a fool. She did not want her affair with Malcolm to become office gossip and, as spontaneous as she had wanted all this to appear to him, had made damn sure that they could not be seen from downstairs. Only if they stood directly in front of the window would they be seen and, as much as she liked the idea, she was certainly not going to do that.

'Now fuck me,' she said.

'What?'

'For Christ's sake, do it.'

Malcolm sprang to his feet, not needing a second invitation. He fumbled with his trousers, unzipping his fly and pushing his pants and his trousers down to his knees. His cock quivered at its freedom.

'Come on,' she said impatiently.

He gripped her by the hips, planted his cock firmly in the mouth of her vagina then drove his hard, strong phallus right up into her.

'Oh God,' Karen moaned, trying to keep her voice down. Malcolm's secretary was right outside the door and hadn't gone home yet. She felt her sex clench around him and this produced a second wave of feeling.

'Come on, fuck me,' she said through clenched teeth. 'I want your spunk in me.' In the future he might not be so lucky. She intended to make sure his ejaculations were strictly regulated, a reward for good behaviour. But at the moment she wanted to feel him coming inside her; she had been thinking about it all afternoon. She dropped her head on to the desk and closed her eyes, concentrating on the feelings as he began to pound into her, his strong muscles pulling her back on him as he thrust forward.

'Come on you bastard, give it to me.' The words excited her further.

She felt his cock swelling and throbbing, both at the same time. He pumped into her so powerfully his belly was slapping loudly against her buttocks, making them tingle. Her labia were stretched apart by the breadth of his cock, exposing her clitoris, and his scrotum was swinging up and hitting it, producing another intense sensation to ratchet up everything else she felt.

He was coming. And so was she, the one orgasm feeding off the other, the feeling of his spunk pumping up into his shaft and his glans ballooning out in the tight confines of her vagina provoking her just as much as her copious juices and the rippling walls of her vagina were provoking him.

'Mistress, Mistress, Mistress,' he muttered as he

slammed into her one last time, his fingers digging into her hips to hold himself there as his spunk spattered out into the depths of her body. And as it did, as she felt the hot gooey liquid jetting into her, she came too, a hard, piercing orgasm that stabbed into her nerves so forcefully she had to stuff her fist into her mouth to prevent herself from screaming.

'Was that what you wanted?' he whispered.

'Yes.' She turned, pulled down her skirt, and walked a little unsteadily to the office door. 'Don't worry, you'll get your reward,' she said.

Chapter Eight

THE DAY AFTER the carpenter finished his work on the special room happened to coincide with the day on which completion of all the legal formalities took place, allowing Karen to call the flat her own. It had taken three weeks. In the meantime she had cleaned and planned the redecoration she was going to do.

With a donation from Malcolm to help her equip the treatment room Karen had written to several specialist suppliers that Pamela had suggested. She was astonished at the range that was available. Not only were there firms making corsets, elaborate bras, panties, suspender belts and outrageous boots and shoes in an enormous range of styles and material, including some corsets fashioned from metal, there were companies that supplied leather bondage harnesses of every description. There were harnesses that could turn a man into a pony, complete with a bridle, reins and a saddle on his back, equipment to enable the hapless victims to be hung fully suspended in a variety of positions, and even cages with thick metal bars, some no bigger than a small fridge. There were cock straps of many different types, and whips, tawses, ferulas and paddles, as well as nipple clips of a dozen different designs.

She also had her own money to spend. With her salary increase and no rent to pay to the Miltons she could afford to buy some of the lingerie from the catalogues and intended, in due course, to buy a lot more. She liked the way she looked in figure-hugging basques, waspies and heavily boned bustiers and plunge fronted bras, and particularly liked red, which went with her long blonde hair. But she liked the way they made her *feel* too. Getting dressed up for sex, preparing herself meticulously with make-up, perfume and lingerie, was a new experience for her but one that never failed to excite her. The ritual of shaving her vulva, which she had adopted religiously, was the same order of thing. Coating her labia and mons with a thick rich lather, razoring it away with sinuous strokes, then slathering the whole area with an expensive silky moisturiser had given them a new importance in her life, made them seem smooth and sleek and pampered, preparing them for the attention that was now their due.

Before, sex had been something she simply did when the occasion arose. She supposed there was something to be said for spontaneity, but if it was spontaneity that had also been carefully planned – like getting Malcolm to fuck her over his office desk – then she could have the best of both worlds.

She had also bought a pair of shoes with the four-inch heels she had seen Barbara and Pamela wear, and though they were difficult to get used to there was no disputing the erotic effect they created, as much on her as on Malcolm.

Malcolm had already visited the flat on several occasions since she had moved in and their sex had been spectacular. Even without the sophistications of the treatment room Karen had discovered that simple everyday items could be just as effective in making sure that he suffered the maximum discomfort should he incur her wrath, which, of course, he inevitably did. She had used washing line to tie him to a kitchen chair and found that this provided not only a good way to straddle him when she wanted to take him inside her, but that if she pushed the chair backward so it was resting on the floor, she could squat down on his face too, without him being able to move a single muscle.

The more she practised the dark arts of domination the more the pleasure she took from it increased. Time after time she had proved to herself, if proof was necessary, that her sexual psyche was powered by deep enigmatic forces that she did not understand but that were defined by the need to have total dominance over men.

Since she had moved out of the Miltons' house she had thought a lot about Barbara. It was Barbara after all who had introduced her to the whole idea of domination and submission. She doubted that she would have had either the courage or the curiosity to react to Pamela in the way she had if she had not already been primed by what she'd seen Barbara doing on the videotape. She also found herself thinking about Barbara's body, those high firm breasts, that slender waist and those plump, puffy labia. Though she had not developed any such feelings for any other women, not even for Tina who liked to parade her young and nubile body in the skimpiest of outfits, the lust she felt for Barbara remained undiminished.

So Karen had decided to take the initiative. To celebrate the transfer of the flat into her name she had planned something rather special. She had made a big salad, bought some excellent French bread, cooked a small salmon and new potatoes, and made her own mayonnaise. Malcolm had donated the champagne that was waiting to be opened in the fridge.

The doorbell rang at five minutes past eight. Karen took the handset of the answerphone from its cradle.

'Come up, first floor,' Karen said, pressing the button that opened the downstairs lock.

Opening the front door of the flat she saw Barbara climbing the stairs. She was wearing a loose cream silk shift dress with spaghetti straps, cream high-heel shoes and sheer flesh-coloured stockings. Her long black hair had been brushed out and flowed around her shoulders.

'Hi.'

They kissed on both cheeks.

'Hey, this is great,' Barbara said as she walked inside.

'Well I've got a lot to do yet. Would you like some champagne?'

'Great.'

They walked into the kitchen together. The shift dress floated around Barbara's slender body and it was absolutely clear that she was not wearing a bra.

Karen opened the champagne and poured it out. They clinked glasses.

'Here's to your new pad,' Barbara said. 'Does it feel very wicked?'

'Wicked?'

'Being a kept woman.'

Karen laughed. 'No, it doesn't. If you want the truth, I'm having a wonderful time. Do you want to eat? I'm starving.'

'Me too.'

They sat at the small table in the kitchen and Karen laid out the food.

166

'You look great by the way, I love that dress,' Barbara said.

The dress was new. It was a tight-waisted scarlet red silk faille with a square neck and an off-centre split in the skirt.

'New,' Karen said.

They soon demolished the food, talking incessantly.

'So how is Dan?' Karen asked as she handed Barbara a second slice of salmon.

'Oh he's just the same as ever. I think he's missing you. Ever since that session you gave him he's been pining.'

'And Jessica?' she asked pointedly.

Barbara's dark brown eyes looked at her steadily. 'She came around last week as a matter of fact. I thought Dan needed a special treat.'

'Does she have a partner too?'

'Oh yes. I told you she likes to organise little parties. Three or four women. And the slaves of course. It can be fun.'

'All together?' Karen said.

'Yes. Jessica can be very imaginative.'

Karen's own imagination was running riot. She pictured three or four men, stripped naked, tied and bound in the centre of the room, while their mistresses, no doubt dressed in the sort of fetishist clothes she'd seen in the catalogues, used and abused them in between bouts of making love to each other.

Karen finished her food. 'Can I ask you something?'

'Of course.' Barbara speared another potato and popped it into her mouth.

'I was rather surprised . . . I mean after I told you about Pamela and me . . . I was surprised . . .'

'That I didn't jump on you?'

'Yes.'

'God Karen, don't you think I wanted to? I used to

167

lay in bed at night thinking about you lying naked in the next room. I couldn't sleep. You're very beautiful.'

'So why didn't you come in?'

'Oh, I suppose it was because I know your mother so well. When we offered to rent you a room it was like she was entrusting you to us. That's why I felt so terrible about you seeing the tape.'

'But I told you what happened with Pamela.'

'Exactly. And I had a hard time convincing myself that I wasn't to blame. I mean, I showed you that tape with Jessica and you go off and do it with a woman. I felt terrible.'

'It wasn't anything to do with you. It was what I wanted. Just like it was with Dan.'

'Karen, I still didn't want to encourage you. Actually, I was furious with Dan for making a pass at you. By the time I'd finished with him next day he couldn't sit down for a week.'

'You didn't say anything.'

'I was very glad that you handled it the way you did, but that didn't mean I was happy with him.'

'Let's have coffee in the sitting room shall we?'

Karen made some fresh coffee and they took it through, settling on the sofa.

'And now?' Karen said, continuing the same subject. 'Now I'm no longer *in loco parentis*?' She reached forward and poured the coffee, handing Barbara a cup.

Barbara laughed. 'Oh, now it's a different story. Now I'm quite happy to tear your knickers off and rape you right here on the sofa.'

'I'm not wearing knickers,' Karen said.

'You're serious aren't you?' Barbara said, her tone changing. Did it contain an edge of excitement?

Karen found it hard to take her eyes off the sight of Barbara's round breasts pressing together under the loose silk, rising and falling softly as she breathed. 'Deadly,' she replied.

'So what precisely do we do about it?' She put her coffee cup down on the table in front of her.

'I tear your knickers off and rape you.'

'I'm not wearing any either, and it certainly won't be rape.'

Karen leant forward and put her hand on her friend's knee. The nylon felt smooth and glossy. She worked her hand up under the skirt. The flesh-coloured stockings had wide lacy tops.

'That feels nice,' Barbara said.

Karen moved her hand higher, up over Barbara's hip and waist. She could actually see her nipples stiffening under the thin silk. The dress was loose enough to let her hand move right up to Barbara's chest. She cupped one of her breasts in her hand, feeling its weight.

Barbara rested her head back on the sofa, staring up at the ceiling. Karen moved her hand across to her other breast, squeezing it, not all that gently.

'Are you going to kiss me?' Barbara said without moving.

'Yes.'

Karen pulled her hand away and knelt up on the sofa, positioning her head above Barbara's. Very slowly she planted her mouth on her friend's lips, barely grazing them. She tasted her lipstick. She ran the tip of her tongue over Barbara's bottom lip but did not push inside. Barbara did not appear to respond. Karen's hand began to move again, down over the silk dress to Barbara's lap. Inch by inch she eased the silk up until she could see the tops of the stockings. Her hand moved down between Barbara's thighs to her smooth hairless mons. She pushed a single finger into her labia but Barbara made no effort to open her legs.

'I'm very wet,' Barbara said. 'I can feel it. If you put your hand in there, you'll feel it.' Her lips moved against Karen's.

'I'm wet too. My juices are running down my cunt.' It was the first time she could ever remember using that word. It gave her a sharp pulse of excitement.

She touched her lips to Barbara's again and let her tongue probe inside. Again Barbara did not co-operate, not closing her mouth against it but not opening it either. It was as if she was trying to decide whether she actually wanted to go on.

Karen dropped her mouth to her neck, sucking on the long tendons that were presented to her, with Barbara's head stretched back. She licked and sucked until she reached Barbara's collarbone. She felt her shudder.

'Yes,' Barbara said, decisively, almost to herself. She sat up, ran her hand around the back of Karen's neck, pulled her face up, crushed their lips together and plunged her tongue deep into Karen's mouth.

Karen pressed her hand down between Barbara's thighs. This time Barbara opened them and Karen's fingers slid down into the furrow of her sex. Barbara was right, she was soaking wet. Karen found the knot of her clit and pressed it back against her pubic bone.

Barbara gasped, the noise expelled against Karen's mouth.

'Lovely,' she said, her head falling against the back of the sofa again.

Karen's finger released the pressure then applied it again, just as Pamela had done with her tongue.

'Lovely,' Barbara repeated.

Without breaking the rhythm Karen slipped down to the floor. She pulled Barbara's legs further apart then knelt between them, pressing forward, until her mouth was inches from Barbara's sex. She could see her puffy labia now, as smooth and silky as her own, and leant forward to kiss them just as a few moments ago she had kissed her mouth, brushing her lips against them then running the tip of her tongue along their whole length.

'God I want you so much,' Barbara said.

'Me too.'

As Karen moved her tongue to replace her finger on Barbara's clitoris, Barbara raised her legs and hooked them over Karen's shoulders, crossing her ankles over her back so her thighs were spread even further apart.

Karen pressed her tongue down on her clit while her fingers probed the entrance to her vagina. The tight tube of Barbara's sex was sticky and hot. She thrust two fingers inside, as far as they would go. There was room for another and she bunched three fingers together this time before pressing them home right up to the knuckle.

Barbara moaned. Her clitoris was throbbing and Karen could feel the walls of her vagina pulsating.

'What are you doing to me?' Barbara said.

Karen's tongue pressed hard, the little button of nerves trapped between it and the hard bone. She ground it slightly from side to side then released it. Barbara trembled.

'You're making me come,' she breathed in a whisper, her body arched now, supported on the back of Karen's neck and thighs.

Just as Pamela had taught her Karen pressed then released the pressure with a rhythm as regular as a metronome. Using the same tempo she sawed her fingers back and forth in Barbara's vagina. But the extraordinary thing was that every tremor of pleasure she could feel coursing through Barbara's body, she seemed to experience just as intensely herself, her clitoris pulsing as energetically as Barbara's and the depths of her vagina responding as if they were being fingered too.

Barbara began to moan loudly and continuously, a low keening noise. Her whole body was rigid now, all of her muscles and sinews stretched taut, all that is bar her clit and the flesh of her vagina which were still fluid and soft and rippling with feeling.

As she thrust her fingers up into Barbara's vagina, Karen felt it contract violently. At the same time her clitoris spasmed against her tongue. Barbara's hands clamped around Karen's head and she came, the moan reaching a crescendo, her body locked as her orgasm racked through every nerve. A gush of juices flooded over Karen's fingers.

Slowly Karen felt the tension go out of her body. She pulled her fingers away and rocked back on her heels, watching as Barbara's sex closed back on itself.

'I didn't expect that this evening,' Barbara said, sitting up. She unhooked her legs slowly from Karen's shoulders. 'You're very good at that.'

'You're very responsive.'

'Now it's your turn sweetie,' Barbara said, leaning forward and running her hands over Karen's arms.

'No,' Karen said. 'There's something else I've got to show you first. Something else you didn't expect.'

'How intriguing. I hope it won't take long. After an orgasm like that I can get very demanding.'

'It won't.'

Karen got to her feet and put her hand out to help Barbara up. Still holding her hand she led her into the hall and up the stairs to the top floor.

'Are we going to the bedroom?' Barbara asked.

'Not quite,' Karen said. She opened the door of the treatment room and switched on the light.

She had decided to paint the room a scarlet red, with a black carpet. The window had been boarded up and covered with a red velvet curtain. The carpenter had constructed a vertical wooden frame in the centre of the room and installed a wooden beam running right across the middle of the ceiling. Malcolm Travers was hanging from a pulley attached to this beam, swinging slightly to and fro. He was naked apart from a leather helmet that covered his whole head, with only two small holes at the base of his nostrils. There were openings for his mouth and eyes but these were closed with small zips. He was strapped into what looked a little like the harness of a parachute, thick leather straps between his legs, around his waist and over his shoulders, fastened to a metal bar above his head, the bar in turn suspended from a white nylon rope threaded through the pulley. His arms were bound behind his back with leather straps at his wrists and elbows. His legs were bound together too at the ankles and knees, his ankles drawn up behind him and a strap firmly binding them to his wrists so his legs were doubled up.

Malcolm's large erection stuck out like a fishing rod. It was encased in a tight cock harness. A strap ran around the bottom of his shaft and under his balls. Another strap was attached to this. It ran between his balls, separating them, and up the whole length of the underside of his phallus. From this at least five other straps banded his cock at one-inch intervals, each cutting deeply into his flesh. The top one was just below his glans.

Barbara examined him closely.

'So this is why he was so keen on you,' she said.

'Mmm . . . he's dishy don't you think? Same sort of body as Dan.' Karen pushed him in the stomach so he swung back and forth more noticeably.

173

'Oh, he's very pretty. And a nice big cock too.'

Karen had seen Malcolm tense at the sound of the strange voice, and his cock twitched visibly. She had not told him what she planned. He had been hanging like this for the last hour.

'As you shared Dan with me I thought I should return the compliment,' she said. She faced Barbara and kissed her lightly on the lips. 'There's a bed over there,' she said, 'if you still want to finish what I started.'

Barbara smiled. 'You've been planning this haven't you?'

'Of course. Shall we let him watch?'

She took hold of the little tongues of the zips over Malcolm's eyes and opened them. She saw him blinking against the light then look at Barbara, taking in every detail of her body.

Barbara returned his gaze. As she stared directly into his eyes she slipped the narrow shoulder straps of the shift dress over her shoulders. It floated to the floor. She was not wearing a bra or panties, just the flesh-coloured hold-up stockings with the lacy tops. Her skin was smooth and lustrous, like the nap of the finest silk, her breasts high and proud despite not wearing a bra, her big nipples knotted into hard buttons of corrugated flesh.

She caught hold of Karen's hand and pulled her into her arms, kissing her hard on the mouth and pressing their bodies together. Karen felt their breasts mashing against each other. Barbara raised her leg, pushing it up until she could flatten the muscle of her thigh against Karen's sex.

'You're a little over-dressed.'

Karen felt the zip at the back of the dress being pulled down. She stepped back and wriggled out of it.

Like Barbara, her legs were sheathed in stockings but they were clipped to a beige suspender belt. She was wearing a three-quarter cup bra in the same material but no panties. The bra fastened at the front. Barbara unclipped it for her, letting her breasts fall free.

'That's much better.'

For a moment Barbara's hand caressed both her breasts, smoothing against them, weighing them in her hand, stroking her palm against the nipples. Then she took Karen's hand again and led her over to the small double bed Karen had installed in the room, its frame festooned with straps and leather cuffs. It was covered with a single white sheet.

'Now where were we . . .'

Karen sat on the edge of the bed while Barbara knelt in front of her. Barbara ran her hands under the blonde's thighs and lifted them up, forcing Karen to lie back on the bed. She hooked her shoulders underneath them and pressed her mouth to Karen's sex.

Karen felt an immediate surge of pleasure. Barbara's tongue lapped at her sex like she was eating an ice cream, long strokes using the whole breadth of her tongue, the little papillae grazing the delicate flesh on the inner surfaces of her labia. Then it bore into her vagina, deeper than she would have imagined possible. She gasped.

Barbara's hands meanwhile travelled up Karen's body and seized her tits, her fingers sinking into the malleable flesh. Then, as her tongue moved up to Karen's clit she centred her thumb and forefingers over her nipples and pinched them hard. The double assault, her clitoris and her nipples both singing with wonderful sensation, created a pulse deep in her sex.

Barbara's hands smoothed down over Karen's body again. She felt one of them travelling under her buttocks and up between her legs, while the other smoothed over her belly and down to her hairless mons. Barbara's tongue was circling her clit as regularly as the second hand on a clock, and though the whole circuit was a cacophony of different delights, there was one place, one tiny bundle of nerve endings on the route, that sent her through the roof with pleasure. Not surprisingly – since Karen's body shuddered and she wailed loudly every time it was touched – Barbara knew just where it was and teased her with it, slowing her tongue just before she approached it, making Karen wait for the shock of sensation.

Karen felt Barbara's fingers playing at her anus. Using the copious juices that had gathered there she slid a single finger into the tight rear passage, right in as far as her knuckle, then twisted it around, all the way around clockwise, all the way back anti-clockwise. At the same time her other hand was flat against Karen's mons, pressing down hard. Her fingers opened out and slipped down on either side of her labia, then pulled back slightly. This had the effect of pulling Karen's clitoris taut and increasing every single feeling it was generating.

'You're making me come,' Karen said, though Barbara could have guessed that from the way her sex was throbbing. She looked at Malcolm, his eyes riveted to the scene, his big cock encased in its unyielding leather harness. The impetus of the push she had given him had just about wound down and his body was almost still. Why seeing him like this, so helplessly bound, excited her so much she still had not been able to work out, but there was no doubt that it did.

'Oh God, Barbara . . .'

Her orgasm crashed through her body. She threw her head back against the mattress and arched her body up as the feelings coursed through her. She had fanta-sised about Barbara doing this to her for a long time but the reality had been even more exciting than she'd imagined. In fact she was so reluctant to allow the feel-ings to leech away, wallowing in the aftermath, that she was barely aware of Barbara lowering her legs to the ground and getting to her feet.

When she finally opened her eyes she saw that Barbara had unstrapped Malcolm's legs so he was standing on the floor, and was busying herself unfas-tening the cock harness. As it fell away Karen saw it had left deep red marks in the gnarled flesh of his cock.

'This is what I want now,' Barbara said.

'Me too.'

She was exactly right. After the soft, delicate minis-trations of a woman's mouth she needed the hard, thrusting penetration of a phallus. Her vagina spasmed at the thought.

Getting to her feet, Karen helped Barbara to unclip the shoulder harness from the metal bar from which it was suspended. They pulled him over to the bed, then pushed him in the chest. With his arms tied so tightly behind him he could do nothing but crash down help-lessly on to the mattress.

Karen jumped on to the bed beside him, straddled him and immediately sunk her sex down on to his big, jutting phallus.

Barbara came up behind her, straddling his legs and pressing her breasts into Karen's shoulders. She ran her hand down to her clit, while the other frotted against her breasts.

'Feels so good,' Karen moaned. The large phallus filled her completely. It was suddenly as though her first orgasm had never gone away, as though it had merely been lurking in her body, ready to spring up again. Within a matter of seconds she was coming, grinding herself down on his cock, while her friend embellished everything by playing her clit and her tits like a musical instrument.

Karen twisted her head back over her shoulder, trying to reach Barbara's mouth to kiss her. As their lips met her orgasm exploded and she was thrown, once again, into paroxyms of pleasure.

'It seems to be my turn again now,' Barbara said, as Karen flopped over on to the side of the bed, leaving Malcolm's phallus glistening with her juices. 'You have got him well trained.'

Barbara took his cock in her hand, squeezed it hard a couple of times, then moved forward and slipped it into her sex, crushing herself down on it. Her whole body shuddered and she moaned as she slowly began to move up and down on it.

It would not be the last time they changed places that night.

'Well what do you say?'

'Yes, Mistress Karen.'

'Yes, what?'

'Yes, I deserve more punishment, Mistress Karen.'

'That's better.'

Malcolm was spread-eagled across the vertical frame, his wrists and ankles strapped into the padded leather cuffs at each corner, the sinews of his arms and legs stretched taut. She had already given him four strokes of a new whip she had bought, one with a thin lash, and his buttocks were criss-crossed with the narrow stripes it left, one of them a bright, almost purple red.

Cruelly she caressed his buttocks, feeling the fierce

heat they were generating, tracing her fingers along the lines she had created and making him squirm in the process. She liked to see that. The more she practised the art of domination the more she had come to enjoy all its recondite diversions. She came around in front of him and traced her finger over his glans, wiping the tear of fluid that had formed there over the smooth pink flesh. For once his cock was not strapped into a harness. She had discovered that the weighted nipple clips she had bought – like the ones Pamela had used on him – could be clipped just as effectively to the loose skin of his scrotum and that is what she had done tonight, the two tear-shaped weights swinging slightly between his legs. If she nudged them with her hand they would swing more energetically, dragging the skin of his scrotum with them.

There always had to be a crime to fit the punishment. She had become an expert in finding imagined slights in the things that he did. When he arrived she would give him little tasks to do that she knew he would be unable to complete. Tonight she had met him at the door wearing a tightly boned red satin corset with a half-cup bra, edged in black satin with dramatic criss-crossing at the front and the back. Her thong-cut panties were red satin too and she wore black stockings and red patent leather ankle boots with a five-inch heel. She had given him the job of cleaning the boots with his tongue. Naturally she had found whole areas that he missed and he had been taken upstairs for his punishment.

Unfortunately for him, on the way upstairs she had caught him staring at her bottom without her permission. That only increased the number of strokes he was due to receive.

'So, four more strokes I think. Shall we use the cane?'

'No, Mistress Karen. Please . . .'

'The cane it is then.'

There was no doubt that Malcolm's obsession with being a slave was just as profound as Karen's with being a dominatrix. And just as she found it hard to fathom why she should get so much pleasure from something so arcane, she could not understand why he was also so addicted to it. Like Dan, the other man she knew with exactly the same predilections, there were no outward signs in his everyday life and he was certainly not deferential or submissive in business. But when it came to sex he was at his happiest grovelling at her feet, often literally, allowing her to take total control of everything that happened. Whatever she did to him, however tortuously she bound him, however hard she whipped him with whichever of the implements she had acquired over the last two months, he was clearly always able to metamorphose the pain and discomfort into a twisted but excruciating pleasure.

It was the same for her of course. Not only had her physical responses been transformed by the discovery of what Pamela had called her sexual nature, the fact that she was now capable of having such intense and overwhelming orgasms made her want to have sex much more frequently. Before, when her lovers had barely been able to give her more than a faintly pleasant flutter of sensation and her own hand had not done much better, she had no incentive to want to indulge in sex more than occasionally. But now, with her mind full of sexually explicit memories and her body so responsive that it could bring her to an explosive orgasm in seconds, masturbation had become not only a startling pleasure but a necessity. She needed sex, and the more her body proved able to give her the most wonderful sensations the more she wanted it.

Karen went to a cupboard the carpenter had built in one of the alcoves of the room, replaced the whip and took out a thin rattan cane. But the tightness of the red satin corset, and the whipping she had already administered, which never failed to arouse her, had combined to create a strong throbbing pulse deep in her sex that was becoming increasingly difficult to ignore. She had masturbated last night with what had become the usual spectacular results, but that was not the same as having him with her, being able to tease and torture him and in the process winding up her own pleasure on his pain. And it had been three days since his last visit.

The trouble with being a dominatrix was that it presented her with so many choices, she thought, smiling broadly, though making sure her face was turned away from her slave. She could do whatever she wanted. And she knew what she wanted to do now. She had collected a selection of dildoes and she took a small straight-sided cream one from the cupboard.

Wiping the smile off her face she tried to look angry as she walked back to the frame. She hooked the handle of the cane over his arm.

'That's to remind you what you're going to get in a minute. But first there's something I need to do,' she said.

She wrapped her arms around his body and pressed herself into him. His big, hot phallus was flattened against the satin panties on her belly. It began to throb, provoking her clitoris to do the same. With the heels on the red ankle boots Karen was taller than Malcolm and had to stoop slightly to kiss him. She plunged her tongue into his mouth and mashed their lips together. This produced an even stronger pulse of feeling in her clit, making it squirm against her labia.

She pulled away from him and drew the satin

panties down her legs, stepping out of them, then cramming them into his mouth.

The dildo had a little switch inset into the flat end on its base. Karen turned it on. The dildo began to hum. She parted her legs slightly and inserted it into her sex. It slid right up without resistance, the juices in her vagina lubricating its passage, until it had disappeared completely. She closed her legs, trapping it in place.

'What are you doing?' he asked, the panties muffling the words, his eyes rooted to her voluptuous body.

'Be quiet,' she snapped. 'Say another word and I'll make it six strokes when I eventually get around to it.'

Her arms slid around his back again and she pressed herself into his strong, hard body. The vibrations deep inside her sex began to spread out, making her clitoris pulse strongly. Her belly was vibrating too and his phallus, ironed flat against it, began to throb aggressively in response. She worked her shoulders, grinding her breasts against his chest, making her nipples, crushed back into the pulpy flesh of her breasts, tingle.

By working the muscles at the tops of her thighs she could push the dildo deeper, then, by relaxing them, allow it to slip down. The movement, though only small, created a panoply of feelings, the vibrations surging through every area of her sex. She felt her sphincter flex so strongly it made her gasp, her anus now almost as sensitive as her vagina.

But she wanted more. Without moving away from Malcolm she snaked her right hand around to her buttocks and down between her legs. She let the dildo slip out of her vagina and unceremoniously jammed it into her anus. With her hand still holding it in place, she eased herself away from Malcolm's body and took hold of his cock with her left hand. She opened her legs and wedged it between her thighs. Stretching up on tiptoe she ground her hips until the tip of his glans nestled into her vagina. Then she lowered herself and felt the hard phallus thrust inside her, alongside the plastic dildo in her rear.

It was a gorgeous sensation. The vibrations of the dildo instantly made his cock not only vibrate but swell too, his glans in particular ballooning out at the top of her vagina. To provoke an even greater reaction she ran her hand down over his buttocks, feeling the raised weals she had created and teasing them, making his body buck and squirm, his cock twisting inside her.

She was coming. The feelings from the tip of the dildo and the tip of his cock seemed to arc together like electricity. She used every ounce of energy to contract all her muscles around both phalluses and was rewarded with a surge of sensation that ran through every nerve in her body. For a second she wondered what it would feel like if the small and cold plastic dildo was replaced by a real phallus, two cocks buried in her at the same time. That thought took her over the brink. Clinging to Malcolm's helplessly bound body, and pressing herself down on his cock, Karen's orgasm coursed through her body, as strong and powerful as anything she had experienced before. In the blackness behind her eyes she saw an image of herself sandwiched between two men, one underneath and one on top.

Pulling away from him, Malcolm's cock was torn from her sex so suddenly it made her gasp. She relaxed her buttocks and allowed the dildo to slip out of her rear, catching it in her hand. This too produced a wave of feeling.

She steadied herself. In all the sexual fantasies she had entertained recently she had never thought of taking two men. Perhaps Barbara could be persuaded to bring Dan around. She wondered if Barbara herself had already experienced that pleasure at one of Jessica's parties.

'Now, where were we?' she said, unhooking the cane from his arm.

She looked down at Malcolm's cock. It was literally dripping with her juices, the two weights hanging from the clips swinging vigorously between his legs.

'Please, Mistress Karen,' he begged through the panties stuffed into his mouth.

'Please what?'

'Please . . .' He indicated his cock with his chin.

'I think I'm going to gag you now,' Karen said.

'Please . . . I can't stand it. Please let me come.'

Karen laughed. 'You're not going to have that privilege for a very long time.' Masochism was a paradox. The more Malcolm wanted relief, the more his body cried out for him to ejaculate, the more pleasure he derived from being tortured and teased.

She stooped and pulled off the clips. He shuddered, trying to shake his cock to ease the pain.

She walked back to the cupboard and took out a rubber ball gag. Pulling her panties out of his mouth she replaced them with the gag and strapped it in place at the back of his head.

'Are you ready?' Before he could answer she stroked the cane down on his buttocks. He produced a muffled cry through the gag.

She raised her arm again.

'How many is that you've given him?'

Karen had her back to the door. She whirled around.

Rebecca Travers stood in the doorway of the treatment room. She looked cool and elegant with her dark brown hair pinned up in a French pleat and her slender body clothed in a coral-coloured silk suit. Her long and beautifully contoured legs were sheathed in natural-coloured nylon so sheer it was almost invisible. She wore coral-coloured high heels with a little silver motif on the toe.

Malcolm began to struggle desperately against his bonds. He made no impression on them.

'You didn't answer my question,' Rebecca said.

Karen felt all the colour drain out of her face. 'Five,' she said, unable to think of anything else to say.

Rebecca walked into the room, closing the door behind her. She was holding a set of keys in her hand. She stood in front of her husband and glanced down at his cock.

'He obviously enjoys it,' she said. She raised her hand and slapped his cock hard with the flat of her hand. 'Do you Malcolm? Is this what you enjoy? Is this why we've barely had sex over the last couple of years?'

Malcolm struggled desperately to free himself.

'Looks like she's done a pretty good job,' Rebecca said, examining the leather cuffs. 'I don't think you're going to be able to get out of that for a very long time.' She looked at him long and hard. 'If you're wondering how I found you it wasn't difficult. You were so careless. The first thing I noticed was the extra keys that had suddenly appeared on your key chain. They weren't for the office or the house so they must have been for somewhere else. So I had a new set made that day you forgot them, remember?' She held up her hand and the keys in front of his eyes. 'Then it was just a case of following you.' She turned to Karen. 'Most nights when he was late I guess he came here straight from work. I'm afraid I wasn't prepared to waste my time sitting around outside the office, so I waited until he was at home and suddenly announced he'd got to go out for a couple of hours, like tonight. Then I followed him. Simple you see. How long has this been going on?'

'Not long,' Karen said, still completely stunned.

'So he had someone before you did he, because he hasn't paid any attention to me for at least two years.'

'I think so.' Karen didn't want to implicate Pamela.

'You seem quite expert at it. Will you show me?'

'Show you what?'

'Show me how to use that?' She pointed at the cane.

'You just swing it,' Karen said, still dumbfounded. She would have expected Rebecca to be wildly angry, but she seemed quite calm.

Rebecca took the cane from Karen's hand. She raised her arm and cut it down on Malcolm's buttocks, so hard his whole body shuddered. A bright red stripe appeared on his bottom. It began to turn purple almost instantly. Rebecca stooped and examined it carefully. She touched it with her fingers, making Malcolm wince.

'Oh yes, that's very good, isn't it? I can feel . . .' Rebecca shuddered. Karen saw a tell-tale spark of excitement in her eyes. 'Why didn't you ever ask me to do this for you?' she said. She slashed the cane down a second time. Malcolm's body went rigid and he tried to scream through the gag.

Rebecca came around in front of him. His cock had began to shrink, but despite the circumstances the pain from the cane revived it again.

'Well, look at that. A miracle. He could hardly get it up with me, you know,' she said to Karen. 'Now I know why. I don't think we're likely to have that problem again.'

'He told me you were going to get a divorce,' Karen mumbled.

'That was probably true. I would have wanted to

divorce him in the end. I need sex. I want sex. And I refuse to have an affair to get it. But now I think I've found the answer, don't you?' She was looking at Malcolm. He nodded. 'Good. Would you mind leaving us now, Karen? No hard feelings. I don't blame you. I'm sure he was very persuasive.'

Karen did not know what to do.

'What are these?' Rebecca said, flicking at the teardrop weights that Karen had left on the floor at the base of the frame.

'Nipple clips.'

'My God,' Rebecca said, picking them up. She opened the serrated jaws and slipped them over her husband's nipples. He moaned loudly as they bit into his flesh. 'I can see I've got a lot to learn.'

She raised the cane then turned to Karen. 'I said you could go now, Karen. Now run along.'

Chapter Nine

'I'M SORRY, THERE'S nothing else I can do,' Malcolm said.

Karen sat in front of the desk that only a matter of weeks ago she had been bending over while Malcolm fucked her. 'I quite understand,' she said. 'If you don't mind I'll leave now.'

'Of course, that would probably be the best thing.'

Malcolm had the grace to look embarrassed at what he was doing. He had told her that his wife insisted that it was inappropriate for him to be working with Karen any more.

'I tried to explain to her, Karen. It really wasn't your fault. I just never realised . . .' He looked across the desk at her. 'I just never realised that she had it in her. All these years I've been going to Pamela, and then I found you. It never occurred to me to ask Rebecca. But you wouldn't believe what she did to me. She's like a different woman, so stern, so commanding. We're going to have a treatment room built at the house. I always thought she was cold and wasn't really interested in sex, but my God she's magnificent.'

Karen did not find that hard to believe. The glint of

excitement in Rebecca's eye as she had raised the cane in the treatment room three days before had been enough to convince her that Malcolm was going to get everything he wanted from his wife and probably a lot more besides.

'I don't really want to hear this Malcolm,' Karen said.

He handed her an envelope across the desk. 'That's one month's pay. I'm sure you won't find it difficult to get another job, and of course I'll give you the best possible reference.'

'Thank you,' she said tartly. The Malcolm that had knelt grovelling naked at her feet, ready to obey her every command, had disappeared. There was no hint of the unique relationship they had shared.

'There's one other thing,' he said sheepishly.

'I know, the flat.'

'Yes.'

'You want it back.'

He looked puzzled. 'It's your flat, Karen. Even Rebecca can't make you give it back. It's in your name.'

'So?' she said.

'I'm afraid Rebecca has insisted I stop making the mortgage payments.'

'But I can't afford to . . .'

'I'm sorry Karen, I really am. But what can I do?'

Karen didn't answer that.

'You won't lose money. If you sell it now you'll be able to pay the mortgage back and still have enough to put down a small deposit on another place.'

Karen got to her feet. 'Is that all?' she said.

'I'm sorry it had to end like this,' he said. 'I just didn't ever dream my wife . . .' The words trailed away.

Karen walked out of his office and down to her desk. She slumped into her chair and began gathering up her personal possessions. She did not blame Malcolm for what had happened; she blamed herself. She had played with fire and had very definitely been burned.

'So what are you going to do?' Barbara asked.

They were sitting at the table in the Miltons' kitchen. Karen hadn't wanted to go back to the flat when she'd left the office so had phoned Barbara and asked if she could come round.

'I don't know. Get a temp job somewhere.'

'And the mortgage payments?'

'Malcolm was right, I'll have to sell. It was nice while it lasted.'

'I'm sorry, sweetie.' Barbara had opened a bottle of red wine. She refilled Karen's glass.

'It was all my own fault. Besides, I don't regret it. I had a wonderful time. It would have been nice if it had lasted a little bit longer that's all. I can't believe Malcolm was so careless with those damn keys.'

'Sounds like she's going to give him a hard time.'

'Oh definitely. I thought he was having trouble sitting down this morning. She's going to punish him for God knows how many years of neglect. But he'll love every minute of it.'

'You've saved their marriage, then,' Barbara said, laughing.

'Better than going to Relate.'

'Look, Dan and I are going to Jessica's tonight. Would you like to come along? I'm sure she wouldn't mind.'

'Jessica's?' Karen raised an eyebrow.

'She's got a new recruit she wanted us to meet.'

'New recruit?'

'I told you Jessica sort of runs this little organisation

190

of people who enjoy the same pursuits. Well, if someone wants to join they have to go through a sort of initiation test. She chooses someone else from the group to help her out.'

'But I don't belong . . .'

'She'd be delighted to meet you, sweetie. I told her a little about you anyway.'

'What sort of thing?'

'Oh, you know . . . just what happened with Dan. And with me of course. I had to tell someone. You don't mind do you?'

Karen wasn't sure. She remembered what she had seen Jessica and Barbara do on tape and felt a little pulse of excitement.

'Come on, it'll be fun. It's just what you need. When you fall off a horse you should get straight back on it again, isn't that what they say?'

'Who's going to be the horse?' She suddenly had an image of the bridle and saddle she'd seen in one of the catalogues of bondage equipment, the tight leather harness fitted around an athletic-looking man on all fours, a saddle on his back and a bit in his mouth.

'You'll have to find that out for yourself.'

'Here we are,' Barbara said. The electric motor of the Rover's window purred as it wound down. An answer-phone was mounted on a post just outside the two large wrought iron gates that were set in a ten-foot high brick wall. Barbara pressed the bell push.

'Yes.'

'The Miltons,' Barbara said.

Karen saw a video camera mounted on the wall to the side of the car move slightly. A second later the gates began to open.

Barbara drove the big car through the gates and into a circular carriage driveway. The house was large and impressive, a Queen Anne mansion surrounded by acres of garden, laid out to lawn, with some huge horsechestnut trees, ancient cedars, carefully planted shrubs and rather formal flower beds. To the left of the main house Karen could see a large conservatory and a swimming pool, and to the right two grooms were feeding the horses in a stable block.

A red Ferrari was parked in front of the house. Barbara parked beside it.

'Very impressive,' Karen said. 'She must be loaded.'

'She is. Big time.'

It had taken an hour to drive out into the country from London but it was still light and Karen could see the newly cut lawns sweeping down to a small lake surrounded by weeping willows.

'Come on,' Barbara said turning to Dan, who was sitting in the back.

Dan reached forward and opened the car door with difficulty. He was naked and gagged, his hands bound together in front of him by metal handcuffs. A chain ran down from these cuffs to the middle of another chain that joined two metal manacles on his ankles. There was a black studded collar strapped around his neck with a metal leash clipped to it at the front. He had spent most of the journey lying flat on the back seat hoping to avoid the prying eyes of passers-by as they drove through the streets of London. He had not alto-gether succeeded, several people spotting him as the car stopped at traffic lights.

As Barbara and Karen got out of the car, Dan managed to pull himself out too. Fortunately they were not far from the front door, as the manacles at his ankles meant he could only take tiny steps and the gravel on the drive cut into his bare feet.

Barbara rang the doorbell.

A petite blonde answered. She was wearing a plain black maid's dress, with a lace apron and a box neck, black fishnet stockings and black high heels.

'Good evening, Ms Milton,' she said.

'Good evening, Olga.'

'This way please.' The girl did not give Dan's naked body a second glance.

The house was as lavish on the inside as on the outside. The hall was lined in cream silk, and large oil paintings, each illuminated by their own light, had been hung along its length. Karen recognised a Kandinsky, a Franz Marc and a Paul Klee, though she was sure the others were also well known. The doors, skirting boards and dado rails had all been stripped back to the original wood and the floor was highly polished oak.

The maid led the way down the wide hallway, past a broad staircase, and through to a pair of double doors. She opened one of the doors.

'I'll take him now, shall I Mistress?' she said to Barbara.

'Of course,' Barbara said. 'Behave yourself Dan,' she added in a stern voice.

The maid caught hold of the metal leash hanging from Dan's collar and pulled him further down the corridor.

Jessica was standing by a huge gothic fireplace in a large sitting room with a glass of champagne in one hand. She was wearing a skin-tight black dress with a high neck but no sleeves. Its short skirt was slit right up to her thigh which was sheathed in sheer and glossy champagne-coloured nylon. Her calf-length shiny black boots had heels so high her feet were almost vertical.

'Darling, how lovely,' she said, embracing Barbara and kissing her on both cheeks.

'This is Karen,' Barbara said.

Jessica's eyes turned to Karen. She was wearing red again, a silk sheath dress with full sleeves and a draped neck. She had brushed her long hair down over her shoulders.

'Oh my dear, you're quite as lovely as Barbara said.' Jessica's hands held Karen's arms as she kissed her on both cheeks too. Quite blatantly she brushed her left hand across Karen's breasts and down to her belly. 'Quite lovely,' she repeated. 'Come and meet Freddie.'

A rather short, slender man was standing by the French window at the side of the room that led out on to a large terrace and the swimming pool beyond. He had thick dark brown hair, brown eyes and a rather delicately boned face, and was wearing an immaculately tailored navy suit with a crisp white shirt and dark blue silk tie. He was, Karen guessed, no more than thirty years old.

'Freddie, this is Karen, and my old friend Barbara.'

'Hey, I'm real pleased to meet you all,' he said with a strong Texan accent. He looked nervous and ill at ease.

'Freddie is an American, as you can hear,' Jessica said. 'Pour them some champagne will you?'

Karen noted that she did not say please.

Freddie trotted over to the large antique cabinet in one corner of the room. He came back with two glasses of champagne.

'He's well trained already,' Barbara said. As Barbara did not say thank you Karen did not do so either.

194

'Yes. Apparently he had someone in New York. She taught him the basics. Is that right?'

'It was when I was very young,' he said. 'I haven't done anything about it since.'

'And now he's fallen into our hands like a ripe peach. Don't look so nervous Freddie, we won't bite.' Jessica laughed. 'Or perhaps we might.' She turned to Karen. 'Keep him amused while I go and check out the arrangements would you? Are you coming Barbara?' she asked, with a rather arch look.

'Yes, lead the way.'

The two women joined hands, walked across the room and disappeared down the hall in the direction in which the maid had taken Dan.

'She's beautiful isn't she?' Freddie said.

'Very.' Karen sipped the champagne. 'So have you been in London long?' She was unable to think of anything else to say.

'Two years now.'

'And you work where?'

'In the City. I do all the London buying on the New York exchange, or most of it anyway.'

'Really? I've always wanted to work in the City.'

'But you don't?'

'No. I've applied for lots of jobs though.'

'You're really keen?'

'Yes.'

'Mmm . . . that's interesting.' He thought for a moment. 'Matter of fact, I have a friend who's looking for a good assistant at the moment. He works for a firm of stockbrokers. Here.' He fished in his jacket pocket, took out a slim black leather notepad with gold corners, scribbled a name and telephone number on a sheet of paper and handed it to her. 'Give him a call will you? You never know.'

'Thanks. I definitely will.'

'He's not into any of this by the way. Just tell him I suggested you called. He's a nice guy, I think you'd get along.'

'Is that your Ferrari?'

'Yes. Bought and paid for.'

'You must be very successful at what you do.'

'I get by. And you? How long have you been involved in this scene? Jessica said it was your first visit.'

'It is.' She left it at that. If Freddie wanted to be a slave then he would have to learn not to ask too many questions.

'Jessica makes me real nervous. She's got a way of looking at you and right through you all at the same time.'

Karen smiled. 'Oh, Jessica is very determined to get what she wants by all accounts,' she said, enjoying Freddie's discomfort.

The blonde maid tapped on the door and walked into the room.

'The Mistress says she's ready for you now,' she said. She walked up to Freddie and held out a collar and chain identical to the one Dan had been wearing. 'You have to wear this,' she said. 'Get down on your knees while I put it on.'

The sight of Freddie getting to his knees stirred something in Karen. She watched as the petite maid wrapped the collar around his neck and buckled it tight.

'Up,' she said, yanking on the metal leash, not at all gently.

Without glancing at the man again she led the way out of the room. They walked down the corridor and through a glass door into what looked like a back addition to the main house.

'You go in there, Miss,' she said to Karen, indicating a door to her right. She took Freddie down to the next door along and pushed him inside.

Karen opened the door. The light in the room was dim and it took a moment for her eyes to adjust. When they did she saw that the room was small and square and painted in a very dark blue. To her right the whole wall was draped with dark blue curtains, while to her left there was a foot-high rostrum. On the rostrum was a double bed, the mattress covered with a single dark blue silk sheet.

Barbara and Jessica were lying on the bed, their mouths locked in a kiss. Barbara had discarded the rather severe maroon suit she had been wearing and was naked apart from a pair of white hold-up stockings with broad lacy tops, and a white lace waspie that was wrapped tightly around her waist but did not cover her breasts. Jessica had abandoned her dress too. She wore a black satin basque with a three-quarter cup bra that lifted her breasts and pushed them together, making them seem bigger than they actually were, and long suspenders that held up her stockings. She had not taken her boots off. Her hand was caressing Barbara's thigh and her smooth shaved sex.

Jessica pulled away from her friend. 'Everything's ready,' she said.

'You'd better explain it to her,' Barbara said, sitting up.

Jessica got to her feet. She came right up to Karen, hooked her arm around her waist and kissed her full on the mouth, squirming their lips together while her tongue explored inside. Karen was startled at how blatant she was, but the surge of pleasure she felt as the woman's body pressed into her own soon overcame

197

her resistance and she kissed her back with just as much vehemence.

'Mmm . . .' Jessica said. 'I like that. I'd like more later.'

'I'm jealous,' Barbara said.

'Don't be. There's enough for everyone.'

Jessica went over to a small cupboard set in the wall by the door. She took out a black velvet bag. 'All right, this is what happens. Freddie wants to join our little circle. Normally we only allow slaves who already have mistresses, but sometimes we make an exception. Occasionally one of our ladies likes to have two slaves under her control, to test one by making them watch her with the other, for example, so it's always handy to have a few spare men.'

Karen nodded. She was astonished at how normal Jessica could make such an arcane world sound.

'But I insist they all pass an initiation test first. We don't want them wimping out later on.'

'And we have a look at what they've got,' Barbara added. 'There's no point if they're not properly equipped.' She winked at Karen.

'When the initiation takes place at one of our parties then the women all draw lots to see who'll put the new man through his paces. So I thought we'd do the same tonight. There's twenty numbered balls. Lowest number gets the prize.'

Jessica held the velvet bag out towards Barbara. She dipped her hand inside and drew out a polished ball about the size of a walnut. It was engraved with the number five.

'Looks like I'm going to be the lucky one,' she said, grinning.

Jessica shook the bag and plunged her own hand

into it. She drew out a ball herself. 'Three,' she said, reading off the number.

'That's cheating,' Barbara said, pouting her lips.

'Perfectly fair,' Jessica said.

She held the bag out for Karen. Karen rummaged around inside and drew out a ball. She held it up. It was number two.

'So it's going to be the new girl,' Jessica said, walking over to the door.

Karen felt a surge of excitement. She had done some extremely unconventional things in the past months but nothing as outrageous as this. Far from feeling intimidated or overawed by Jessica's assertiveness, however, she felt nothing but fascination and arousal in her presence. Now it looked as though she wasn't just going to be a spectator in whatever Jessica had planned but a participant.

'What do you want me to do?' she asked, breathily.

There was a circular switch on the wall by the door and Jessica turned it. Immediately the blue drapes began to part, revealing a huge floor-to-ceiling glass panel.

On the other side of the glass was a square room with walls swathed in scarlet drapes. In the middle of the floor was what looked exactly like a four poster bed except that it had no curtaining and the frame was made from plain, very thick wood, inset at regular intervals with metal rings. The mattress of the bed was covered in a black sheet.

Dan Milton stood at the foot of the bed facing inward. His handcuffs had been stretched up to the crosspiece that ran between the top of the two corner posts and hooked into a metal ring at its dead centre. The metal manacles had been separated from the chain that had once joined them and were now locked to metal rings at the bottom of each corner post so his legs were forced apart.

The blonde maid was in the process of fixing Freddie to the other end of the bed, kneeling at his feet securing his left ankle, his wrists and other ankle secured in exactly the same way as Dan's. He had been stripped naked and his cock was already starting to engorge.

The maid got to her feet and looked directly into the glass panel. Karen guessed it was probably a one-way mirror and all she could see from that side was her own reflection.

'Does that excite you?' Jessica asked. She came up behind Karen and ran her hand down over her breasts. If she was feeling to see if Karen's nipples were erect she was not disappointed. They were as hard as stone.

'Yes.'

'Looks like he's very fit,' Barbara said, nodding toward the glass. The maid had finished his bondage and Freddie's cock was now fully erect. He was uncircumcised but the foreskin had retracted halfway over his glans. His body was muscular and covered with a mat of thick dark brown hair. Karen noticed that Barbara's hand was frotting lazily against her hairless sex.

'All right Karen, it's up to you. Go and show him what being a slave is really about. We'll be watching.' Barbara kissed her neck, so delicately it made Karen's flesh pucker with goose pimples.

Karen stared at the two men. She knew at once what she was going to do and the thought made her shiver with excitement.

'Unzip me,' Karen said, turning her head over her shoulder to look at Jessica.

Jessica found the tongue of the zip and pulled it all the way down to the small of Karen's back, then brushed the shoulders of the dress down so it fell to the floor. Karen stepped out of it. Like Barbara she had paid a great deal of attention to her lingerie. She was wearing a black basque made from some new material which was not only pliant and flexible, clinging to her body like a second skin, but glossy and almost transparent. The seams and the curved boning that emphasised her narrow waist, and the underwiring and edging on the low cut bra, were all faced in black satin. At the hem of the garment the material extended down in four narrow triangles, hanging from which black satin suspenders supported her equally glossy black stockings. Her long legs were shaped and firmed by her black leather high heels. She was not wearing panties and her smooth mons and the slit of her labia underneath it were clearly visible.

'Mmm . . . that's nice,' Jessica said. Karen wasn't sure whether she meant her body or the basque.

'Is there anything I should know, or do I just follow my instincts?' Karen asked.

'The maid is there to help you.' Jessica replied. 'Everything else is up to you.'

As Jessica went back to join Barbara on the bed, Karen walked out of the door and out into the corridor. She opened the next door along and found herself facing a scarlet drape. Pulling it aside she strode on to what she knew to be a stage, with Jessica and Barbara watching everything she did.

She had been right about the one-way mirror; most of one wall of the room was taken up with it, the whole room reflected. In one corner of the same wall was a rack of various implements of flagellation, and shelves of other equipment, bondage harnesses, gags and blindfolds in rubber and leather together with coils of white nylon and hemp rope.

'Good evening, gentlemen,' Karen said.

She studied both men carefully, walking around the bed. It had been some time since she had seen Dan in this position but it was clear that he had lost none of his enthusiasm for submission, his large cock quivering as it stuck out from his belly. Freddie apparently shared the same fervour, his erection just as prominent. They were both staring at her hungrily, their eyes roaming her body, their heads turning to follow her every movement.

She went up to the rack of whips and picked out a riding crop with a braided leather handle. Instead of the usual loop of leather at its tip, however, the crop tapered down to a very thin thread with a tiny knot at the end. She swished it through the air and saw Freddie flinch.

'Well, we'd better get started,' she said, glancing into the mirror and imagining Jessica and Barbara lying on the bed watching her. She walked up to Dan. 'Did I give you permission to look at me?' she barked.

'No, Mistress Karen.'

'No, I did not. And you?' She looked across at Freddie on the other end of the bed. 'Did I?' There always had to be a transgression to punish.

'No, Mistress Karen,' he intoned in his American drawl.

'Then you will both have to be punished, won't you?'

They said nothing.

'When I ask you a question I expect it to be answered.'

'Yes, Mistress,' they both mumbled.

'That's better.'

Karen ran her hand over Dan's buttocks. It was quite clear that Barbara had treated him to a beating in the last few days as there were vivid red and scarlet stripes across his bottom.

'The only question now is who is going to go first?'

The excitement that she had felt the very first time she had seen Dan bound and dominated by Barbara was a thin shadow of what she was feeling now. Exercising total power over two strong, handsome and totally powerless men willing to obey her every command was driving Karen wild. She could feel her clitoris throbbing and her sex moistening, her hard nipples pressing out against the tight material of the basque. It was her initiation too, she knew, a sort of rite of passage. She had to prove to Jessica that she deserved to be treated as an equal. Then she might be invited to join Jessica's little circle; if these were the sort of games they played that could prove to be very interesting.

She moved over to Freddie, standing behind him. Unlike Dan his neat, lean buttocks were unmarked. Virgin territory. Pressing her body into his back she squirmed her breasts against his shoulder blades while her hand snaked around his hip and grabbed his cock, yanking back his foreskin to reveal the whole of his glans. He moaned.

'You first I think,' she said.

She stood back, raised her arm and swung the crop down on his rear. He yelped like a dog.

'Be quiet,' she snapped.

She cut another blow down, intersecting the first. Freddie's whole body shook but he managed to stifle his cry.

'That's better,' she said.

The sound of leather against flesh reverberated

around the small room. She gave him three more strokes then glanced towards the mirror, letting Barbara and Jessica see the excitement she knew was making her eyes glint.

'One more,' she said. But before she delivered it she ran her hand over his buttocks, torturing the red-hot flesh, her fingers tracing each raised weal. Freddie shuddered violently and let out a long, low hiss through clenched teeth. 'Is this what you want?' she whispered in his ear.

'Yes, Mistress Karen.' There was no doubt that it was true. In the mirror she could see his cock twitching frantically.

She raised her arm and swung the crop down again, watching as it cut deep into his flesh and made his whole bottom quiver. The effect on her was no less dramatic, her sex rippling with sensation and her clitoris pulsing so strongly it took her breath away.

'What do you say?'

'Thank you, Mistress Karen,' he said.

Throughout this the maid had stood placidly at the side of the room, watching what was going on but with apparently no reaction.

'I want him lying on his back on the bed,' Karen said, addressing her for the first time. 'Tied down nice and tight.'

The maid nodded. She came over to Freddie, took a little key from her pocket and reached up to free the handcuffs.

'Now, what about you,' Karen said, coming back to Dan. 'I see Barbara's had to punish you.'

'Yes, Mistress Karen.'

Watching Freddie take six strokes of the riding crop had only increased Dan's excitement. She could see that his whole body was quivering with arousal, a sticky wetness dripping from the end of his glans down on to the black sheet.

Karen raised the crop. Thwack. Dan's buttocks were fleshier than Freddie's and vibrated more. Thwack. Thwack. Every stroke made Karen's sex contract sharply. She could feel a deep rhythmic pulse begin to spread from her vagina to her clit and out through the rest of her body.

Wanting to give Dan exactly the same treatment as Freddie, she stopped after the fifth stroke and caressed his bottom with her hand. He moaned softly, trying to press himself back against her. His buttocks were radiating heat.

As the maid manoeuvred Freddie on to the bed in front of them, pulling his arms up above his head and strapping them into leather cuffs at each corner, Karen raised the crop one last time. The final stroke was the most savage of them all and made Dan cry out loud.

Dropping the crop on the bed Karen took hold of one of Freddie's ankles, pulling it to the corner post and strapping it into the leather cuff that hung there. The maid did the same with the other ankle. They adjusted the chains that held the cuffs so his whole body was stretched and taut.

Karen put her high-heeled shoe on the edge of the bed right beside his head. One of the sheer black stockings had wrinkled slightly at the knee so she bent forward and used the palms of both hands to draw the nylon up from her ankle to the thigh until it was perfectly smooth. She unclipped the suspender, adjusted it to make it tighter, then pressed the little rubber button into the metal frame of the suspender clip, trapping the sheer nylon again. Freddie's eyes were glued to her sex. She was so wet she could feel her juices had leaked out over her labia and was sure they were glistening wet.

'Did I give you permission to look at me?' she snapped.

'No, Mistress Karen,' he said, visibly shrinking away from her as far as his bonds would permit.

'Do you like what you see?' she said more softly. Without putting her foot down she stroked the whole length of her labia with a single finger.

'Yes, Mistress Karen,' Freddie said in a whisper.

Karen knelt up on the bed, then swung her thigh across his shoulders, her buttocks resting on his chest, her sex inches from his face.

'Then you'd better take a closer look,' she said. She pressed the whole of her hand down between her legs and pulled back, spreading her labia apart with her fingers. 'Can you see it all now?'

'Yes, Mistress Karen. You're beautiful,' he said breathily.

'Do you know the rule, Freddie?'

'No, Mistress Karen.'

'The rule is that you are not allowed to ejaculate unless and until I specifically tell you to. Is that clear?'

'Oh no,' he wailed.

'Oh yes. If you do then I don't imagine Mistress Jessica's going to allow you to join her little, club do you?'

He shook his head. 'I can't,' he said. 'I can't do it.'

'You have to,' she said.

Still holding her labia apart she eased herself forward until her sex was an inch away from his mouth.

'Come on, lick my clit now.'

He raised his head and flicked his tongue against the

206

little pink button of flesh. Then he pushed it gently from side to side. Karen felt a huge pulse of feeling sweep through her body.

'Very good, perhaps you're not so useless after all,' she said, pressing her sex down against his mouth, the lips of her vagina sucking at the hard bone of his chin.

He established a rhythm, the tip of his tongue hardly moving at all but causing huge paroxysms of pleasure in her body. He was good at it, his tongue applying just the right pressure in exactly the right place. Already the deep throbbing feeling that had begun as she whipped them was joining the feelings he was creating to form a more profound pulse. But it was not only the physical distractions that were driving her wild; the idea that not only was she here with two men but that beyond the glass Jessica and Barbara were watching everything she did, added to her excitement. There was something else too, an idea that had gnawed away at her since she'd first been told that she was going to be able to use the two men. Whether she'd have the courage to do anything about it was another matter but the thought alone was making her come.

As Freddie's tongue worked relentlessly at her clit Karen felt her orgasm explode. It raced from her clit to her vagina then up through her body, the constriction of the tight basque somehow increasing the force with which it lanced through her nerves.

But Karen wanted more. Even before the last tremors of feeling had faded away she slid down his hairy body, her sex leaving a trail of wet on his chest, until she felt his cock nudging into her gaping labia. She reached around her back, grabbed his phallus and slammed it unceremoniously into her vagina, thrusting herself down on it at the same time. She sat up straight and ground her hips, wanting to get him as deep as he would go.

Coming on top of her first orgasm, the penetration caused an immediate shock of sensation. The whole of Karen's sex clenched around the rock hard sword of flesh, while her clit, trapped between their bodies, let out a quake of feeling so intense she thought she would come again. But she steadied herself and tried to concentrate. Lifting her body she allowed him to slide almost to the mouth of her vagina.

'I can't, I can't,' he moaned, tossing his head from side to side.

'Shut up,' she said. 'You don't have any choice.'

Freddie looked up at her. His mouth and chin were coated with her juices. 'Please . . .' he said pathetically.

Karen looked at the maid. She could easily have brought herself off again like this. It would have taken a matter of seconds. But she wanted more.

'Cut him down,' she said, nodding in Dan's direction.

The maid did as she was told. As she freed Dan from the metal rings that bound him to the bed, Karen eased herself back down on Freddie's phallus. She wished she had thought to torture him with nipple clips, like she had done so often with Malcolm, or strap his cock into a leather harness, but her own feelings had got the better of her. Slowly, making sure she did not provoke herself too strongly, she sawed her vagina up and down on him, his cock slippery with her juices. She looked into the mirror. What were Jessica and Barbara doing now?

Dan stood at the side of the bed, massaging the tops of his arms.

'Get up here,' she said.

He knelt on the bed.

'Behind me.'

She felt him settle himself behind her, his knees on either side of Freddie's legs, his big hot cock nudging against the cleft of her buttocks.

'All right, Dan. I want you to bugger me.' The words themselves made her shudder with excitement.

His hands grasped her hips immediately. He pulled his cock back slightly then pushed forward so it was centred on the perfectly round hole of her anus.

Karen sunk herself all the way down on Freddie's cock. As Dan prodded forward she felt a wave of sensation as sharp as anything she had felt before. The ring of muscles at her anus felt as sensitive as her clit, and the heat and smoothness of his glans made it throb with just as much feeling. In her mind's eye she could actually see it, butting against her puckered round hole, while below Freddie's cock stretched the mouth of her vagina wide apart.

Dan thrust his erection forward. Karen's sphincter gave way and he slipped inside her rear. It was tight. The presence of Freddie's cock in her vagina had made the opening in her anus that much smaller, and even though only Dan's glans had penetrated her the pain was so intense she thought she was going to faint. She screamed out loud and threw her head back against Dan's shoulder.

She would have to stop. She simply could not stand it. Their cocks would split her in two.

But the waves of pain rippling through her body changed subtly. Her vagina, clit and her nipples were the first to register a new sensation, a prickling, stabbing sensation that was on the same frequency as pain and certainly just as intense, but was very definitely pleasure. Before she had realised what she was doing, unconsciously she began to push herself back against Dan's body.

His cock slid an inch deeper. Again there was a huge shock of unmitigated pain, but the gap between this and the hard-edged pleasure that followed it was much shorter.

Dare she? Dare she?

'Deeper, push it deeper,' she said, twisting her head so she could look Dan right in the eyes.

She felt his fingers digging into the soft flesh of her hips again, then he pulled his buttocks back, and used them as the motor to drive his cock right up into her anus.

Karen screamed, but not from pain. This time there was no gap between the explosion of pain and the rush of pleasure, the two feelings coming together, so inextricably mixed that they formed something new. She had felt the same sensation before when Malcolm had buggered her, but this was on a different scale. She could feel both cocks deep inside her, hard, hot and throbbing, separated only by the thin membranes of her own body.

'Yes,' she said triumphantly.

Dan began to move in her, pumping back and forth. But she wanted more than that now.

'Come on Freddie, fuck me,' she demanded.

Freddie's face was lined and fearful, his muscles and sinews rigid with the effort of trying to stop himself from coming. 'I can't,' he said. 'Please . . .'

'Do it.'

Karen felt him buck his hips. As Dan's phallus withdrew Freddie pushed forward. They slid against each other, turning the membrane that separated them into a new erogenous zone that erupted with feeling.

The tightness of both passages of her body meant that Karen could feel every inch of the cocks that were buried in her body and distinguish every feature. In the cramped and crowded space, the distinct ridge at the bottom of the glans seemed to be catching on some inner dimension as they both sawed back and forth, creating two spikes of monumental pleasure.

Dan's hand had reached around her back and was grasping at her tits, pinching at her nipples one after the other, as if there was not enough sensation flowing through her body.

She was coming now. She had never felt anything like this. The mental stimulation matched the physical on every level. Not only was this was forbidden and taboo, a breach of all decent behaviour, which gave her excitement an added twist, it was also something she had fantasised about since that first time she had used the dildo and Malcolm's cock together in her body. And she only had to glance to her left and see it all in the mirror, her body sandwiched between the two men, the black basque and the stockings completing an erotic image that burned into her mind as powerfully as a glance at the sun burns into the retina of the eye.

The pain gave her pleasure new meaning. But as it drove her towards orgasm she felt Freddie's cock beginning to kick and throb violently against the tight confines of the silky wet vagina that surrounded it. She could actually feel his spunk pumping up from his balls.

She didn't care. She wanted it.

'Don't you dare,' she said, because she was in control and she wanted to assert her authority.

His cock jerked violently. He thrust up into her with all his might, despite the weight of two bodies bearing down on him, and Karen felt as though the very top of her vagina had blossomed like a flower, creating a space for his glans to pulse and kick and jet out gobs of red-hot spunk.

But the feeling of Freddie's cock throbbing so violently right next to his own set Dan off too. With Freddie still trembling under the impact of orgasm Dan's cock began to throb, the tightness of her rear almost strangling the movement. As he slammed himself forward, his belly slapping against her buttocks, his spunk jetted into her too.

Karen had been coming from the moment she'd felt Freddie's cock start to pulse. Whether she had come as his spunk spattered into her and again as Dan had lost control, or whether it was just one long continuous orgasm she had no way of knowing. All she did know was that she had never felt anything like it before. The nerves at the back of her eyeballs had forced her eyes closed again. She had thrown her head back and was making a long low noise that was more like a rattle somewhere in her throat than a moan. Inside her the copious spending of two men made her whole sex feel molten, like the centre of a volcano, every twitch and pulse of her clit and vagina producing new waves of pleasure almost as extreme as her orgasm itself.

The sensations had been so intense that when she finally opened her eyes again it was almost like waking from a deep sleep. She had trouble remembering where she was. It was only when she looked into the mirror that it all came flooding back.

'You know what that means don't you,' she said in a voice that was too weak to sound as threatening as she intended. 'It means you're both going to have to be punished.'

But not yet she thought. Not yet. Even that orgasm had not left her sated. She knew exactly what she wanted now. And the extraordinary thing was that she knew she only had to walk into the next room to be assured of getting it. And in spades.

'Come in,' she said.

Freddie walked through the door. He looked nervous and ill at ease. 'I brought you some champagne,' he said.

Karen did not acknowledge the gift. 'You're late.'

'The traffic was bad.'

'Don't make excuses,' she snapped. 'Get upstairs and get stripped. I want you on your knees on the floor with your hands behind your back, do you understand?'

'Yes, Mistress Karen,' he said.

'Do it then.'

Freddie Bartholomew began to run to the stairs.

'Give me the champagne.'

He retraced his steps and handed her the bottle.

'Now go.'

He vaulted up the stairs, taking them two at a time.

Karen smiled. She walked into the kitchen and looked at her watch. Her next visitor wasn't due for half an hour. Plenty of time to get Freddie into bondage before she arrived. She'd have a glass of champagne first. After all, these days she had a lot to celebrate.

Judd Bernard was American. He was six foot five and wore snakeskin cowboy boots to the office. Karen had been working for him for two months. She had called him the morning after her visit to Jessica's house, as Freddie had suggested, and he had interviewed her and given her the job the next day. She was, he had told her there and then, exactly what he was looking for. What's more, the salary was almost double what she had been getting at the agency. It was without doubt the best job she'd ever had in her life. He was good at delegating and the more he found her capable of, the more he gave her to do.

Bernard and Cooper was a small firm of stockbrokers specialising in looking after the European interests of their mostly American clients. Karen had quickly learned the intricacies of investments and the stock market and was enjoying every minute of it. She had never been exactly sure why she had wanted to work in the City, but now she knew her instincts had been proved correct.

She had not expected to see Freddie Bartholomew again after the night at Jessica's, at least not without Jessica or one of her little circle in attendance, but two days after going to Jessica's house he had turned up at her front door with a bottle of Krug champagne. He'd got her address from Judd he explained and hoped she'd allow him to celebrate her new job. It had been pretty obvious what he really wanted.

After his second visit, when he'd seen the For Sale sign outside the flat, he'd asked her why she was going to sell. She explained about Malcolm Travers and his wife and that she could no longer afford the mortgage, even with the hike in salary that Judd had given her.

Freddie couldn't bear the thought of losing the delights of the treatment room and had offered to take Malcolm's place in every sense. If she were prepared to have him as her slave, he would see the mortgage payments were met. What's more, unlike Malcolm, Freddie Bartholomew was not married.

The arrangement was working out well. Freddie was an obedient and devoted slave. Jessica had taken the news that Freddie was no longer a 'spare man', to be given to the other ladies in her little circle, with equanimity, though that was not surprising.

214

After Freddie's initiation had been completed Karen had fallen into bed with Barbara and Jessica and enjoyed another bout of extraordinary sensual pleasure. But it had rapidly become clear that Jessica had developed a strong passion for her. Subsequently she had twice asked Karen to her house on her own and had pleasured her in very much the same way that Karen had seen her pleasure Barbara on the tapes. Karen was quite sure that even if she was annoyed that she had stolen Freddie so quickly, she would not want to mention it for fear of jeopardising their relationship.

Karen poured herself a glass of champagne. She was wearing a silk robe over her red satin basque with the criss-crossed black lacing, flesh-coloured stockings and high-heeled red open-toed slippers with a tuft of boa feather on the toe.

She sipped the champagne then took her glass and climbed the stairs. She began to feel her own excitement mount. She was looking forward to what she had planned for this evening.

Freddie was waiting in the treatment room exactly as she had ordered, naked on his knees with his hands clasped firmly behind his back. She wondered if she would ever get used to the flush of excitement she got when she saw a man bowing to her will.

'So what shall we do with you tonight.'

He had told her he had got involved in domination and submission in New York, where he had gone to a club that specialised in such things. He had met one woman who had claimed to be a dominatrix but who had not, according to him, been very strict with him at all. Only after his initiation at Jessica's house had he realised how much he had to learn.

Karen took hold of the white nylon rope hanging down from one of the overhead pulleys.

'Stand up,' she ordered. She went over to the cupboard and extracted a pair of black rubber briefs. 'Put these on.'

Freddie scrambled to his feet and pulled the black rubber around his loins. His erection tented the front of the tight material.

Karen tied the rope around his wrists then hauled it through the pulley until Freddie's arms were held almost vertically behind him and he was forced to bend forward at right angles to his legs.

'Spread your legs apart.'

He obeyed with difficulty, afraid of losing his balance. Karen took out a leg spreader, a metal bar with a leather cuff at each end, and strapped the cuffs around his ankles. She forced a gag into his mouth, holding his lips apart, then fitted a black silk sleeping mask over his eyes.

'Very good,' she said. She slapped her hand down on his rubber-covered buttocks. 'What do you say?'

'Thank you, Mistress,' he tried to say, but the words were indistinct. She could see his cock quivering under the rubber pants.

The doorbell rang.

'I've got a surprise for you tonight, Freddie,' she said.

He tried to raise his head but the cramp in his shoulders was already too great.

She closed the door and walked downstairs, pressing the button on the answerphone that unlocked the front door. A moment later there was a knock on the door of the flat.

'Darling, how are you?' Pamela said, as Karen threw open the door.

'I'm wonderful. God it's good to see you again.'

'You too.'

Pamela looked magnificent. Her big body was clad in a leather catsuit which fitted her like a second skin. Her fleshy breasts ballooned out of its low V-neckline where a zip ran all the way down the front of her body to her crotch. The leather was so tight it had folded itself into the slit of her sex. As usual she was wearing ultra-high heeled leather calf-length boots.

They kissed. It was meant to be a brush of the lips but it became something more meaningful, their tongues dancing together as their hands smoothed over each other's bodies. Karen felt Pamela's breasts flatten against her own, her nipples stiffening instantly.

'Mmm . . . that's a nice start to the evening,' Pamela said.

'There's more where that came from. I've missed you. The champagne's open.'

They walked through to the kitchen. 'So how's business?' Karen asked, handing her a glass.

'The same as ever. It never ceases to astonish me just how many men want to be slaves.'

'Or how many women want to dominate them.'

'I'll drink to that. And what about you? How's your love life after that little rat Malcolm?'

Karen had told Pamela all about Malcolm on the phone. She grinned. 'Come and see for yourself.'

She led the way upstairs. 'This looks familiar,' Pamela said as they reached the door of the treatment room. Karen had painted it black.

'It seems a long time since I walked through a door just like this,' Karen said.

'It is.'

'I didn't know what I wanted then.'

'And you do now?'

'Yes.' She kissed Pamela on the lips again. 'Everything. And what's more, I know how to get it.'

Karen opened the door to her treatment room, ushered Pamela inside and closed it again after them.